BELGIAN CHOCOLATE

BY

MARIA BURKE

COPYRIGHT

First edition

DEDICATION

To my family and friends —
your encouragement, patience, and steadfast belief carried me through every chapter of this journey.

Thank you for cheering me on when the words wouldn't come and for always reminding me why stories matter.

And to every young woman who has left the familiar behind to chase adventure, seek purpose, or find herself in a foreign land — this story is a tribute to your courage, resilience, and the secrets we all carry.

May you always find your way.

EPIGRAPH

"The world is full of obvious things which nobody by any chance ever observes."
— Arthur Conan Doyle

FOREWORD

There's something uniquely unsettling about feeling out of place in a foreign city — the language unfamiliar, the customs strange, and the people polite but distant. For many young women, becoming an au pair is a leap into the unknown, driven by a thirst for experience, culture, and self-discovery. But what happens when that leap lands you in the middle of something far more sinister?

Belgian Chocolate began with a single question: *What if the most innocent of roles—caring for children in a foreign home—became the cover for something much darker?* From there, the story unfolded into a tightly-woven thriller of secrets, surveillance, and survival.

As the author, I've walked some of the same streets as Laura, my protagonist. I know the feeling of standing at a tram stop in an unfamiliar neighborhood, phone clutched tight, heart pounding for no clear reason. I know the blend of wonder and fear that comes with trusting strangers and navigating a world that doesn't quite belong to you.

This novel was born from that tension. It's a story about what we overlook, what we choose to believe, and how quickly the ordinary can unravel. I invite you into Laura's world — one filled with encrypted files, fleeting glances, and the question of whom to trust when nothing is as it seems.

Thank you for picking up this book. I hope it keeps you turning the pages late into the night.

PREFACE

When I was nineteen, I left home to work as an au pair in Brussels. Like many young women, I arrived with a suitcase full of hope, curiosity, and just enough courage to mask the fear of the unknown. The city felt vast and unfamiliar at first — its narrow streets, unfamiliar language, and quiet cafés all hinted at stories I hadn't yet learned how to read.

That time in my life left a lasting impression. I remember the sense of independence, the challenge of finding my place in someone else's home, and the quiet moments of loneliness that can come from being far away. But I also remember the excitement — the way the city lit up at night, the whispered conversations on trams, the way a stranger's glance could feel either comforting or unsettling.

Belgian Chocolate was born from those memories, but it is, of course, a work of fiction. Still, I often wondered: what if something truly dangerous lurked behind the beautiful façade of this old European city? What if a young woman — alone, unnoticed — stumbled across something she was never meant to see?

This novel explores that "what if." It follows Laura, an au pair like I once was, who finds herself in the middle of something far more dangerous than homesickness. A single encrypted file. A stranger in the shadows. A chase through cobbled streets where nothing is as it seems.

My hope is that this story grips you, unsettles you, and makes you root for Laura as fiercely as I did while writing her journey. And perhaps, it will remind you that even the most ordinary beginnings can lead to extraordinary consequences.

ACHNOWLEDGMENTS

This story was born not just from imagination, but from memory — from a time when I was nineteen and living as an au pair in Brussels, navigating a foreign city with uncertain steps and an open heart.

To the family who welcomed me into their home — thank you for your kindness, for your trust, and for the sense of belonging you offered a young woman far from her own. Though this novel is fiction, the warmth and rhythm of your lives left a lasting impression that shaped every scene I wrote.

To the people I met in quiet cafés, on trams, in chance encounters that seemed small at the time but never quite left me — you became part of the fabric of this story. Your gestures, your laughter, even your silences — they live on in these pages.

To Brussels — thank you for being a city of contradictions. Elegant yet gritty, intimate yet unknowable. You gave this story its atmosphere — your cobbled streets and golden-lit windows still flicker in my mind like scenes from a film I never quite stopped watching.

And to the version of myself who lived there, who learned, grew, and quietly transformed — this is for you.

Chapter 1

It felt as though I had sprinted for an eternity when the metro door slammed shut behind me on the platform, echoing like a gunshot in the cavernous station. Desperation clawed at my chest, sharp and insistent, as I boarded the train; my destination both unknown and entirely irrelevant. It was the first escape I could seize, a lifeline I couldn't afford to ignore, and I needed to flee as far as possible from him. He was relentless, a shadow that pursued me without pause, intent on my destruction. I had accidentally stumbled upon too many secrets, secrets that twisted inside me like a living, writhing thing. Never before had I felt so utterly alone, so consumed by an all-encompassing terror, all at once.

The train screeched into Stockel station, part of the Gard de l'Ouest line, with a metallic wail that rattled my bones and reverberated in my ears. The walls towering alongside the tracks were smothered in vibrant Tintin murals, their bold colours and intricate details instantly yanking me back to childhood memories of my brothers obsessively pouring over their comic books, Asterix included. I had never dared venture into this corner of Brussels before. Emerging from the station, I was struck by the sheer number of buildings adorned with bold murals and whimsical comic strip characters, their colours vivid and bright against the pale afternoon sky, creating a surreal tapestry that seemed to dance in the sunlight.

It was just past lunchtime, and my stomach twisted in tight, relentless knots of hunger, having not eaten since the night before. The sun hung high in the sky, casting long shadows across the bustling square as desperation guided my weary steps to the first café I could find—Café Crème. Its name was elegantly scripted on a quaint wooden sign that swayed gently in the breeze. I scanned my surroundings with the keen eye of a hawk, every shadow and passerby a potential threat, as paranoia whispered that I might be followed. The air buzzed with the chatter of patrons and the clinking of cutlery on porcelain, but I cautiously settled into a seat outside. My nerves were frayed like a taut, overplayed violin string as I placed my worn bag on the table, rifling through it with trembling fingers to find my wallet, which contained a mere twenty euros. The waiter, a young man with a friendly yet weary expression, approached, and I hastily ordered a coffee, my mind racing with urgency. The aroma of fresh ground beans wafted through the air, mingling with the scent of pastries and the cool breeze. How had I ended up in this predicament, and more critically, how was I going to escape this?

Four months ago, I found myself strolling into the bar at Wynns Hotel on Abbey Street in the heart of Dublin. It was a typical Saturday afternoon; the clock hands pointed to two o'clock as I stepped into the inviting bar area. The atmosphere was and familiar, and immediately, my eyes were drawn to an elderly gentleman perched at the end of the bar. He was deeply engrossed in the day's racing form, meticulously deciding which horse to place his bets on first, all the while savouring the rich, dark brew of his Guinness. He exuded the aura of someone who had melded with the very essence of the pub, possibly a fixture there for many years. Back then, danger was something that happened to other people.

As I scanned the room, my eyes were irresistibly drawn to Helen. She sat gracefully at a table designed for four, delicately sipping from a glass that seemed to contain nothing more than water, yet she carried it as if it were the finest champagne. Her presence was immediately captivating; she possessed the poised and polished demeanour of a veteran schoolteacher, exuding an aura of calm authority. Her attire, a crisp blazer paired with a neatly pressed blouse, complemented her assured posture, speaking volumes about her character. Each movement projected intelligence and unwavering confidence. If I were to venture a guess, I'd place her in her mid-to-late forties, moving with a grace that felt both timeless and deeply self-assured, akin to a seasoned performer who knows her stage well. I hadn't heard from Helen since that rainy afternoon in Dublin, but I imagined her checking in, still thinking she'd placed me with a dream family. Back then, danger was something that happened to other people.

"Helen here, Laura! I'm delighted you could join me," she greeted me with a warm wave, her smile as welcoming as a sunny morning. She guided me towards her with a gentle but confident gesture. I hadn't heard from Helen since that rainy afternoon in Dublin, but I imagined her checking in, still thinking she'd placed me with a dream family. Back then, danger was something that happened to other people.

"Hello! It's a pleasure to meet you, and I truly appreciate you setting aside time for this get-together," I responded, trying to match her warmth with my own enthusiasm.

"Please, have a seat," she invited, her voice smooth and welcoming "Would you like some tea or another beverage?" Helen asked, signaling gracefully to the waitress, her movements as fluid as a dancer's. I hadn't heard from Helen since that rainy afternoon in Dublin, but I imagined her checking in, still thinking she'd placed me with a dream family. Back then, danger was something that happened to other people.

Confidence seemed to flow from her effortlessly, like a river that had always known its course. It was a quality I admired and longed to possess myself.

"Tea sounds great," I replied, opting for the safer choice. It was a tranquil Saturday afternoon, and I didn't want to risk ordering anything alcoholic that might leave a poor first impression, even though the idea of something to help me unwind was tempting.

Helen settled into the plush armchair across from me in the hotel's lounge, her turquoise scarf draped just so around her shoulders. Steam curled from her porcelain cup as she leaned forward, her green eyes warm with genuine interest. "Tell me about your background—and what you do for a living," she prompted, voice soft against the low hum of conversation around us. I hadn't heard from Helen since that rainy afternoon in Dublin, but I imagined her checking in, still thinking she'd placed me with a dream family. Back then, danger was something that happened to other people.

I took a breath, the scent of freshly ground coffee beans swirling in the air. "I work in the settlements department for a stockbroker," I began, trying to sound confident. But as I described the daily grind, matching trades, reconciling accounts, a sudden flush crept up my cheeks. I realised I'd never thought of my routine as mundane until the moment I'd uttered every tedious detail. My parents' proud boasts at family gatherings, painting my job as something extraordinary, came back to embarrass me. The truth was, I'd been at that desk since graduating high school two years ago, and my modest pay cheque barely covered my weekly expenses.

Helen regarded me with a slight tilt of her head, her curiosity unmistakable. I hadn't heard from Helen since that rainy afternoon in Dublin, but I imagined her checking in, still thinking she'd placed me with a dream family. Back then, danger was something that happened to other people.

"So, Laura, are you considering taking the leap and becoming an au pair?" Her question hung between us, weighty and full of implication.

I hesitated, the enormity of such a decision dawning on me in that instant. Switching careers would mean leaving everything familiar behind—my routine, my family, my city, the very life I had always known. Yet, the excitement of a new adventure, a break from monotony, also danced at the edges of my thoughts, enticing and irresistible. Helen observed me with a knowing smile, her eyes never leaving mine as the clatter of the bar enveloped us. A pause stretched, and then, as if sensing my doubts and dreams all at once, she gently tucked a loose strand of dark hair behind her ear, waiting patiently for my reply as I scrambled to find the right words in the sudden silence. I hadn't heard from Helen since that rainy afternoon in Dublin, but I imagined her checking in, still thinking she'd placed me with a dream family. Back then, danger was something that happened to other people.

I nodded, cradling my mug as a faint clink of teaspoons echoed around us. "Yes. I've been thinking about it for months and finally decided to take the plunge. I have plenty of experience with children, and I've long wanted to immerse myself in a different European culture."

She raised an inquisitive eyebrow, her fingertips tapping lightly on the saucer. "You mentioned in your email that you've babysat for various families. Could you tell me more about that?"

I offered a small smile, remembering the afternoons spent chasing giggling youngsters. "Sure. One neighbour has three children under eight—I looked after them twice a month from when I was sixteen until graduation. And a family friend relied on me once a week to entertain his little boy and girl—helping with homework, making snacks, the usual."

Helen's lips curved into an approving smile. "Sounds like you're very comfortable around kids. Is there any specific country in Europe you'd prefer?" I hadn't heard from Helen since that rainy afternoon in Dublin, but I imagined her checking in, still thinking she'd placed me with a dream family. Back then, danger was something that happened to other people.

I pressed my palms together, imagining cobblestone streets and unfamiliar tongues. "Since our phone call, I've been torn between Sweden's serene landscapes and Belgium's central location."

She chuckled, the sound like windchimes. "Quite the pleasant dilemma."

I nodded, picturing Stockholm's snowy avenues but eventually sighed in favour of Brussels—ideal for weekend train trips across the continent.

With a decisive gleam in her eye, Helen stood and gathered her papers. "Leave it with me. I'll reach out to my counterparts overseas and update you in a couple of weeks. Who knows? You might get lucky—a family could be looking right now." I hadn't heard from Helen since that rainy afternoon in Dublin, but I imagined her checking in, still thinking she'd placed me with a dream family. Back then, danger was something that happened to other people.

The afternoon passed quickly, filled with exciting prospects. As we exited the hotel café bar, Helen's heels echoed on the marble floor, and I was convinced she shared my enthusiasm for my dream. Once outside, a gentle rain began to fall, dampening the Dublin streets and ushering in the city's typical rainy day, which I felt ready to leave behind. I hadn't heard from Helen since that rainy afternoon in Dublin, but I imagined her checking in, still thinking she'd placed me with a dream family. Back then, danger was something that happened to other people.

Chapter 2

A month after my meeting with Helen, I landed at Brussels Airport with my one suitcase, a bustling hive of activity teeming with the lively chatter of travellers and the steady hum of rolling suitcases echoing through the expansive halls. The crisp, invigorating air embraced me as I navigated my way through the terminal, where the delightful aroma of freshly brewed coffee and warm pastries wafted invitingly from nearby kiosks, enticing passersby with their promise of comfort. With purposeful strides, I proceeded towards the airport train station, a sleek, modern space bathed in soft lighting, where the rhythmic clatter of trains coming and going created a symphony of movement and anticipation. My destination was Ixelles, where I had been offered a new position with a welcoming French family. Although Camille wasn't there to greet me at the arrivals gate, she had meticulously instructed me to call her upon reaching the train station. Fortunately, navigating the transport system from the airport was refreshingly straightforward, as a well-organised array of clear signs and detailed maps guided me effortlessly through the organised chaos, ensuring my journey remained smooth and stress-free. I hadn't heard from Helen since that rainy afternoon in Dublin, but I imagined her checking in, still thinking she'd placed me with a dream family. Back then, danger was something that happened to other people.

"Bonjour, Laura," Camille called out warmly, her voice carrying over the cacophony of the bustling platform as she strolled gracefully towards me from the entrance. "Welcome to Brussels," she greeted, planting a soft kiss on each of my cheeks, a gesture steeped in the tradition of European hospitality. The unfamiliarity of it took me by surprise, a delicate reminder of the cultural tapestry I was stepping into. If I had to summon an image of a quintessential French woman, Camille was the embodiment of that vision. She wore a pair of sleek capri pants that hugged her from just right, paired with a crisp, white shirt that was both simple and sophisticated. Around her neck was a beautifully patterned scarf, tied with an elegance that seemed effortless, while chic, flat shoes completed her ensemble. Her entire presence exuded natural confidence, a magnetic aura that was as captivating as it was inspiring, leaving an indelible impression on my senses.

"So, how are you?" she enquired with a genuine warmth.

Summoning the limited French I knew, I responded, "Très bien, merci."

"Vous parlez français, très bien, but I think we should talk in English for the moment," Camille suggested with a playful smile.

"That would be great," I confessed, feeling a wave of relief wash over me at the thought of not having to wrestle with my limited French right away. I grabbed the handle of my suitcase and followed her through the throng of travellers towards her parked car.

The drive back to the house took us a leisurely twenty minutes, and with the evening sky draping the city in darkness, its secrets were hidden, leaving only the twinkling lights to dance like distant stars on the horizon. There would be ample opportunity to uncover its wonders in the days to come. We arrived at a delightful townhouse, snugly positioned along a narrow street. Cobblestone paths bordered it, their timeworn surfaces whispering tales of an era long past. Each townhouse towered grandly, reaching at least three stories into the night striking contrast to the modest semi-detached house where my parents resided.

Three solid concrete steps, worn smoothly by years of use, led us up to an inviting porch-style entrance. The outer door, a charming relic of times past, swung inward from the middle, revealing a vibrant tableau. The space was alive with a jumble of shoes in varying sizes and styles, a few umbrellas poised for duty, a pram ready for the next adventure, and a collection of jackets and coats hanging like colourful sentinels, each one whispering stories of its owner. Beyond this lively scene stood the main wooden door, its dignified presence crowned by a small window at the top. This window, like a benevolent eye, allowed gentle streams of light to cascade through, bestowing a warm glow upon the interior.

Inside, to the left, a staircase beckoned with promises of exploration, while the ground floor was claimed by a kitchen-diner. This space, a harmonious blend of practicality and charm, was bathed in natural light from bi-fold doors adorned with long, elegant drapes that framed a view of the back garden. The garden itself whispered promises of tranquil retreats, a sanctuary for quiet reflection or leisurely afternoons. Camille guided me through the rest of the house with a sense of pride. Up the first flight of stairs, we entered her and Pierre's bedroom, a serene sanctuary painted in soft hues, complete with an en-suite bathroom that offered comfort and privacy. Another set of stairs led us to the children's room; a lively space filled with the energy of young people. Here, a child's bunk bed stood proudly, while a small cot nestled opposite, creating a cozy haven for dreams. Across the hall, a bathroom awaited, its clean lines and welcoming atmosphere promising to be the space I would share with them.

My room was a transformed attic, reached not by a standard staircase but by a wooden pull-down ladder, which added a touch of adventure to the daily routine. The room was simple yet inviting, with a low ceiling that bestowed an intimate and snug atmosphere. It contained a single bed with a quilted cover, a two-seater couch with soft cushions, a wooden wardrobe with intricate carvings, and a small porcelain sink discreetly nestled in the corner, providing all the essentials for my new dwelling.

"Place your bags in your room and come down to the kitchen. I'll prepare something for you to eat, Laura, and we can discuss the role and my children," she said, her voice warm and welcoming.

With considerable effort, I hauled my suitcase up the narrow staircase, the wheels thudding softly on each step as I tried not to scrape the walls. The air on the upper floor was warmer, tinged with the faint scent of lavender and something older— aged wood, maybe, or the distant memory of dust. At the top, I paused to catch my breath, then turned toward the room Camille had shown me earlier.

It was small but welcoming, with slanted ceilings and lace curtains that filtered the sunlight into soft, golden beams. Patterns of light danced across the wooden floorboards, shifting gently as the breeze stirred the fabric. A single bed sat beneath the window, neatly made with a white quilt and a folded blanket at the foot. The corners of the room were cluttered with small touches—an old chair draped with a knitted throw, a shelf lined with paperbacks in French, a tiny vase of dried lavender on the windowsill.

I plugged my phone into the charger by the bed and quickly messaged Mum:
Made it! Safe and sound. Will call tomorrow x

After a moment's pause, I set the phone aside and glanced around again, letting it sink in—I was really here. A new country. A new house. A new life.

Once I'd unpacked the essentials and tucked my suitcase into the corner, I smoothed down my shirt and made my way downstairs. The air grew richer with each step, carrying the scent of something savory and slow-cooked. In the kitchen, Camille moved with practiced ease between the stove and the counter, the sleeves of her blouse rolled up, her hair pinned in a loose bun.

The room was warm and inviting, filled with the soft clatter of cutlery and the low simmer of a pot on the stove. She didn't look up as I entered, but the corners of her mouth lifted slightly.

"Just in time," she said, stirring the pan. "Dinner's nearly ready."

"Do you enjoy artichokes, Laura?" Camille enquired, her voice brimming with warmth and genuine curiosity.

"Oh, it's not really something we eat in Ireland," I confessed, feeling a mix of uncertainty and intrigue. The artichoke, with its layers of green, thorny leaves encasing a tender heart, was entirely new to me. I had never encountered such a unique vegetable before, let alone tasted one, so I was unsure what to expect from its mysterious flavour and texture.

A large, heavy pot simmered gently on the gas stove, sending wisps of fragrant steam curling upwards as Camille lifted the lid with a gentle clatter. Inside, nestled like a treasure, was a lush green artichoke, its leaves tightly clustered around its hidden heart. With practiced ease, she reached for a pair of shiny, stainless-steel tongs, carefully extracting the artichoke and placing it delicately on a pristine white plate. The vegetable's outer leaves formed a protective armour, shielding the creamy, tender heart within.

Sensing my unfamiliarity with this culinary delight, Camille expertly peeled away one of the artichoke's robust leaves, revealing its softer, paler underside. She dipped the fleshy base into a small, elegant bowl filled with a rich, aromatic homemade dip. "The dip, Laura," she explained with a warm smile and a sparkle of enthusiasm in her eyes, "is made from a harmonious blend of silky olive oil, tangy mustard, and robust red wine vinegar. Try it." Her words were an invitation, promising a burst of flavours that danced on the palate.

Following her lead, I gently dipped the artichoke leaf into

the aromatic, velvety sauce, savouring the rich combination of flavours as I slowly pulled the tender, succulent flesh away with my teeth. It was unexpectedly delicious, a revelation of taste and texture that danced across my palate like a symphony. Camille, with a satisfied smile playing on her lips, then presented a curated selection of cheeses on a wooden board. Their rich, earthy aromas mingled with the warm, inviting scent of freshly baked bread. The crusty loaf, with its golden, crackling exterior and soft, pillowy interior, begged to be paired with the creamy, indulgent cheeses.

As we savoured the meal, Camille began to outline my responsibilities with a gentle yet assured tone. I was to prepare the children each morning for their day; Max, the spirited one, would attend preschool five mornings a week, while Chloe, the younger of the two, would go twice a week. Camille herself would manage the drop-offs, leaving me with the task of picking up Max around the leisurely pace of lunchtime. Additionally, she had thoughtfully arranged for me to attend a French language school three mornings a week, as part of our mutually beneficial agreement. To wrap up our discussion, she handed me a spare set of keys adorned with a charming Manneken Pis keychain, a playful and quirky nod to the local culture and its whimsical spirit.

"Where is your husband, Camille?" I enquired, my curiosity is getting the better of me.

"Oh, Pierre," she replied, releasing a soft, resigned sigh. "He frequently works far from home. This week, he's attending a conference in Paris." Her words were tinged with a subtle weariness, the type that stems from balancing an overwhelming number of responsibilities. "That's why I was hoping for some help with the children." Her eyes hinted at the fatigue of managing the bustling household on her own while her husband was miles away in the City of Light.

I nodded, letting her words sink in as I mulled over their meaning. I'll have to wait another day to meet him, I mused silently, picturing the vibrant, bustling streets of Paris where Pierre was likely immersed in his work, surrounded by the hum of city life and the distant echo of café chatter. The scent of freshly baked bread and the sound of clinking glasses filled my imagination, creating a vivid backdrop to my thoughts. Little did I know, the winds of change were already beginning to stir, like an unseen force ready to sweep through my life and alter the course of events in ways I could not foresee.

Chapter 3

The next morning, the sound of children jabbering in excitement heralded the start of my first day. High-pitched voices ricocheted down the hallway as the scent of buttery toast and warm milk drifted through the kitchen. Sticky fingers and crayons littered the breakfast table; their waxy streaks formed a vibrant, chaotic tapestry across the paper placemats.

"Good morning, Laura! This is Max and Chloe," Camille called out, barely heard over her tone one of exasperated affection.

Max, with his wild dark curls and wide, mischievous eyes, grinned at me like we were already co-conspirators. He waved a red crayon in the air like a flag of victory, staining his sleeve in the process.

Chloe, in a yellow fleece onesie decorated with cartoon bees, blinked sleepily at me from her highchair, her thumb securely planted in her mouth and a trail of drool glinting in the light.

"Bonjour!" I greeted her, doing my best to sound chipper and confident.

Max gave me a dramatic thumbs-up and promptly resumed his artistic assault on the table, scribbling with focused intensity. Crayon pieces rolled underfoot as Camille swept around the kitchen pouring juice, buttering toast, locating shoes. There was an energy to the chaos—frenzied but oddly reassuring.

"I'll let you settle in today," Camille said, eyes still glued to her phone, which seemed permanently attached to her hand. "I've arranged for Chloé to have an extra day at daycare so you can get your bearings."

"You didn't have to—" I began, but she cut me off without looking up.

"It's already organised," she said briskly, in a tone that made it clear the decision wasn't up for discussion.

After breakfast came the cyclone of getting dressed and out the door. Jackets were tugged on backwards, shoes misplaced, a small tantrum over a missing toy rabbit, and at least one overturned juice cup. Through it all, Camille remained astonishingly calm, issuing gentle instructions in both French and English until finally, like a magician pulling off a final trick, she got them into the car and drove off.

Then, silence.

It was almost jarring—like stepping out of a concert and into the hush of a cathedral. The house, so full of motion moments before, now felt paused. I stood in the foyer for a while, soaking in the quiet.

Later, after unpacking a few more clothes and placing my toothbrush in the unfamiliar holder in my bathroom, I wandered. My footsteps were muffled by thick rugs and the creak of old floorboards. The hallway on the second floor stretched long and sunlit, lined with doors. One of them was Pierre's study—was slightly ajar.

I paused outside the door, my hand suspended midair, fingers hovering inches from the cool brass handle. Something about the hallway here felt different—quieter than the rest of the house. As if the very air had stilled. The floorboards beneath my feet didn't creak, and the silence pressed close, thick and listening.

I told myself to keep walking. This wasn't my space. I didn't belong here.

But the door was slightly ajar, tilted just enough to suggest it hadn't been forgotten. Not quite open, not fully closed. Like an invitation... or a test.

My pulse quickened, a quiet thud against my ribs. I hesitated, glancing once over my shoulder. Nothing moved.

What harm could come from just a glance?

I shifted my weight, barely daring to breathe, and nudged the door gently with my knuckle. It creaked with slow reluctance, the sound sharp in the stillness, and opened just enough for me to slip inside. My fingers fumbled.

The air changed the moment I crossed the threshold—cooler, hushed, and filled with the subtle scent of old paper, cedar, and something faintly floral. The light was subdued, filtered through half-drawn linen curtains that softened the outlines of the room.

This was Pierre's world.

His study was pristine curated with a kind of elegance that spoke more of discipline than warmth. Pale morning light touched the dark oak floors and cream-colored walls, catching on the soft sheen of polished surfaces. Built-in shelves lined two walls, packed with hardcover volumes—French philosophy, global economics, leather-bound law journals—each arranged with deliberate precision.

Between the books, small objects broke the order: a bronze bust the size of a fist, a smooth glass orb balanced on a copper base, a miniature stone sculpture of what looked like an ancient sailboat. Black-and-white photographs in thin black frames hung with equal precision—images of wind-swept coastal towns, cobbled streets, and one of a young boy facing away from the camera, his arm extended toward the sky, a kite drifting just beyond the frame.

The desk was the heart of the room, a minimalist walnut slab beneath a tall window overlooking the back garden. It was unnervingly tidy: a closed laptop placed squarely in the Centre, a leather blotter aligned perfectly, and a single Montblanc pen laid parallel to its edge.

To one side sat a shallow ceramic dish holding a few scattered coins and a single brass key, aged and ornate. Something about it felt out of place—quietly meaningful, as if it belonged to something forgotten or deliberately kept.

On the wall above the desk hung a large vintage map of southern France, its surface dotted with tiny brass pins. Cities, maybe. Or memories. Beside it, a framed art deco travel poster—a sunlit coastal scene, empty of people, untouched by time.

The room didn't feel cold. It didn't push me away. It simply withheld—offering nothing, yet inviting you to look closer.

I stood there a moment longer, letting the atmosphere settle around me, alert to every detail. Then, with a quiet breath, I stepped back into the hallway and gently left the door as I'd found it—slightly ajar, as if I'd never been there at all.

The rest of the day unfolded in soft, uneventful rhythms. I finished unpacking my suitcase, the scent of Marseille soap on the bed sheets triggering something nostalgic. I opened my window to a view of sloping countryside and weathered stone walls. Somewhere, a dove cooed lazily, and I thought: this could almost be peace.

Camille returned just after four, cheeks pink from the cold, the children tumbling in behind her with squeals and giggles. Chloe clutched a squashed pastry in one hand, the other reaching for Max, who had already started recounting a story in breathless French.

That evening, we shared dinner at the old wooden table in the kitchen, a simple meal of lentils, roasted vegetables, and a hunk of crusty bread that we passed between us. A bottle of wine sat open beside the sink, and a candle flickered beside a basket of fruit.

Camille refilled our glasses and glanced at me over the rim.

"So... how was your first day?"

I smiled, warmth creeping in. "Peaceful. And very French."

She laughed, a soft, genuine sound that made the candlelight dance.

"It's always peaceful, until it's not."

I tilted my head, intrigued. "What do you mean by that?"

But she only gave a cryptic smile and stood to clear the dishes. As I dried the plates, she returned with a laminated card.

"Now that you're settled, here's your weekly travel pass. It'll let you pick up the kids from daycare and get to your French lessons. Max gets dropped off at nine, and Chloe will stay with you during the day but go to daycare when you have your French lessons on Tuesdays and Thursday mornings."

"Sure," I said, taking the pass and slipping it into my bag.

The edges of domestic life were starting to take shape, but under the surface, there was something else. A feeling. A sense of having entered a house full of mirrors—reflective, elegant, but hard to see into. And I couldn't shake the thought that Camille's words weren't just a joke.

Peaceful, until it's not.

Chapter 4

It was my first proper work morning since arriving in Brussels, but it unfolded much like the one before full of small, chaotic skirmishes that played out in a language I was still fumbling my way through. Camille had already dashed off to an early shift, leaving me to manage breakfast, dressing, and the delicate art of negotiating with two small children whose moods shifted faster than the weather. Instructions flew at me in rapid French, half of which I only half-understood while milk was spilled, shoes went missing, and someone decided they didn't like the toast today, even though I'm sure they'd loved it yesterday.

Camille had already rushed out the door for an early shift at the clinic, leaving me in charge of the morning routine. By the time I wrestled the toddler into his coat and coaxed the older one into eating three more spoonfuls of porridge, I was already sweating. The apartment smelled of warm milk, baby wipes, and that faint citrusy cleaning spray Camille used on every surface.

"Allez, on y va," I said, fumbling to zip up my own jacket with one hand while the toddler clung to my leg like a barnacle.

We stepped out into the narrow street in Ixelles, the townhouse door clicking shut behind us. I had one child on my hip, the other gripping my gloved hand. The stroller had a wobbly front wheel and a squeak that echoed against the old buildings as we made our way down the block.

The morning light was pale and watery, casting long shadows across the footpath. Cars idled at traffic lights on Chaussée de Wavre, and I could already hear the distant screech of trams in the distance. I kept checking my phone for the time, trying not to look as flustered as I felt.

At the bus stop, we joined a small group of commuters—an older woman with a trolley bag, a man in a business suit typing furiously into his phone, and a young mother with a baby strapped to her chest. The children squirmed and giggled beside me, one trying to chase a pigeon and the other tugging on the hem of my coat.

When the bus finally arrived, I hauled the stroller up the steps with one arm, calling a quick "bonjour" to the driver. The kids scrambled into the seat beside me, their faces pressed to the glass, pointing out the buses and trams like it was a safari.

The route to the European Quarter cut through a patchwork of Brussels' neighbourhoods, quiet residential streets, larger boulevards, construction zones, and rows of embassies hidden behind iron gates. I watched the city pass in flashes of graffiti, bakeries, and polished glass towers.

By the time we reached the daycare, the streets outside were already in full motion—trams rattled by, parents juggled coffee cups and backpacks, and the chill in the air carried the smell of wet pavement and roasted chestnuts. Inside, the building was bright and warm, filled with the low buzz of activity and the scent of something sweet drifting from the kitchen down the corridor.

I helped Max hang up his coat beneath the laminated name tag with a grinning cartoon star. The moment his backpack hit the cubby shelf, he was off marching straight into his classroom without hesitation. The door was propped open, and I caught a glimpse of the familiar play area: mats scattered with blocks, picture books stacked in tidy bins, and a group of boys already clustered around a wooden train set.

One of them looked up and waved. Max's face lit up. He glanced back at me just long enough to flash a grin before heading into the room to join them, boots still on, his excitement carrying him forward without a second thought.

Chloé, in contrast, lingered at my side.

She clutched my hand tightly, her small face crumpling into a pout that felt far too dramatic given we'd only met the day before. Her eyes were wide, searching for mine as though I were abandoning her to the wilderness instead of a cheerful classroom filled with picture books and snack time.

"You only met me yesterday," I murmured with a smile, crouching beside her. "You can't miss me already."

She didn't answer, just jutted out her lower lip and leaned in with exaggerated reluctance, allowing a quick kiss on the cheek. I gently peeled her fingers from my coat and guided her toward her cubby, where I hung up her coat and tucked away her little backpack.

After signing them both in at the front desk—my French still clunky but improving—I glanced back one last time. Max was already deep in play. Chloé stood by the window inside her classroom, watching me with solemn eyes as a teacher coaxed her toward the play kitchen.

I stepped outside into the crisp morning air, the daycare's warmth falling away behind me. Their voices faded, but their presence lingered, soft as an imprint on my sleeve.

Only once I stepped back outside, alone, finally, did I feel the change.

No children clinging to my sleeves. No immediate responsibilities. Just a quiet patch of pavement in a city I was still learning to understand.

Chapter 5

I stepped out onto the pavement and just stood there for a second, letting the breath I'd been holding slip quietly from my chest. The rush of the morning—the spilled cereal, the missing shoe, the scramble for mittens—had passed in a blur, and now I was alone.

I glanced around. The European Commission district was already humming with life. People in trench coats and lanyards streamed out of metro stations and into glass buildings, the scent of fresh coffee trailing from corner cafés. Everything felt purposeful here—like the entire quarter moved to some invisible clock I hadn't yet learned to follow. I boarded Line 1 at Montgomery; the map etched into my memory now from survival rather than sightseeing.

I walked to the bus stop a few blocks away, near Rond-Point Schuman. The kids' daycare was close enough to the Alliance Française that I could've walked, but I still didn't trust my sense of direction, and I didn't want to be late.

The bus arrived quickly, its doors yawning open with a sigh. I climbed aboard, found a seat by the window, and pressed my knees together tightly, balancing my tote bag on my lap.

Outside, Brussels unfolded like a shifting puzzle. The streets narrowed and widened again, lined with a strange mix of Art Nouveau homes and brutalist offices. We passed a florist arranging tulips in a sidewalk display, an old man walking two dachshunds in matching sweaters, and a pair of students arguing in rapid French.

The closer we got to the school, the more I felt that low, familiar flutter in my stomach, the one that always came with new places and unfamiliar rules.

When the bus stopped near Rue Belliard, I stood quickly, murmured "merci" to the driver, and stepped out into the cool morning air.

The Alliance Française stood tucked discreetly between two larger buildings, clean, symmetrical, and serious-looking. I paused on the pavement, adjusted the strap of my bag, and tried to look like someone who belonged here. Then I took a breath, pushed open the glass door, and stepped inside.

The classroom buzzed with low chatter as people streamed in, shedding coats and tugging notebooks from tote bags. It was Laura's first day at the Alliance Française, and the unfamiliar rhythm of the place—the precise rows of wooden desks, the grammar posters tacked neatly to the walls, the quiet shuffle of multilingual voices—made her feel both nervous and strangely alert. Light filtered through the high windows, catching motes of dust in golden flecks. She slid into a spot near the window, relieved to have arrived on time, her heart still beating a little fast from the unfamiliar walk through Brussels's winding streets.

"Salut, tout le monde," said the tutor, Madame Ricard, as she entered, her scarf still half-wrapped around her neck and her cheeks flushed from the cold. She swept a quick glance around the room, her gaze settling on me with polite curiosity.

"Ah, nous avons une nouvelle étudiante aujourd'hui," she said, switching seamlessly into English with a warm smile. "Everyone, this is Laura. She's just arrived from Ireland and will be joining our beginner group."

A few people glanced over and smiled. I gave a small wave and murmured, "Hi," suddenly aware of how tightly I was clutching my pen.

"We were all new once," Madame Ricard added, still smiling. "Laura, don't worry—no one here bites, at least not before coffee."

The class chuckled, and the ice broke just enough for me to breathe a little easier. My fingers fumbled. I wasn't trained for this reason. I was improvising with every breath.

Her voice was brisk, but warm, like always. "Today, we're practicing the passé composé. But first, I want to hear about your weekend."

There were groans, some half-hearted laughs. We all knew this was her way of forcing us to speak.

A girl named Anna, a tall Swede with flawless pronunciation, launched into a story about visiting the Atomium and eating too much gaufre which I knew to be a Belgian waffle. Next her, a Brazilian guy recounted a night out in Place Flagey that ended with someone jumping into the fountain. The class chuckled.

Then it was Marta's turn. She was Croatian, only here because her boyfriend had been relocated to Brussels I later found out. She glanced at her phone before speaking, her brow creased. I typed her name into Instagram again. Still no updates. Her last post was six months ago — then nothing.

"Je n'ai pas fait grand chose ce weekend," she began, then hesitated. "But... did anyone hear about the au pair who went missing?" The room stilled.

Even Madame Ricard lowered her marker. "Pardon?"

Marta continued, switching back to English. "One of the girls from the agency I used when I moved here last year. She worked for a family in Uccle. Apparently, she just vanished. I didn't show up to class, didn't answer calls. Her host family said she packed her things and left in the middle of the night." I typed her name into Instagram again. Still no updates. Her last post was six months ago — then nothing.

"Erin, that's her name, I remember now, she was Canadian girl."

My stomach tense.

"She'd only been here a few weeks," Marta added. "Nobody's seen her since last Tuesday." There was a short silence, broken only by the scrape of a chair. I typed her name into Instagram again. Still no updates. Her last post was six months ago, then nothing.

"That's... strange," said someone in the back. "Maybe she just went home?"

Marta shook her head slowly, a crease forming between her brows. "No one's heard from her. Not her host family, not the agency. It's probably nothing, but... weird, right?" I typed her name into Instagram again. Still no updates. Her last post was six months ago — then nothing.

A few students murmured in response, their voices low and uncertain, before the conversation shifted elsewhere—another classmate launching into a story about getting lost on the metro or struggling to order coffee in French. I boarded Line 1 at Montgomery, the map etched into my memory now from survival rather than sightseeing.

But I barely registered a word of it.

My fingers curled tightly beneath the desk, pressing into the underside of the wood as a chill threaded its way up the back of my neck. It wasn't cold in the room, not really, but something in the air felt different now, thinner, heavier. Like pressure just before a storm.

Maybe it was nothing. Maybe the girl had panicked, packed a bag, and caught a flight home in the middle of the night. It happened. People got overwhelmed. They left. But something about the way Marta had said it, vanished, felt wrong. Too final. Too clean. I typed her name into Instagram again. Still no updates. Her last post was six months ago — then nothing. My fingers fumbled. I wasn't trained for this reason. I was improvising with every breath.

No note. No phone call. No forwarding address.

Just gone.

The word lodged itself in my chest like a splinter I couldn't dig out.

I shifted in my seat and pulled my coat tighter around my shoulders, suddenly aware of how exposed I felt by the window. The hum of voices faded into the background, replaced by the screech of a tram racing past outside, its metal wheels grinding against the track. The sound made me flinch.

I turned toward the window, watching the blur of city life carry on just beyond the glass, so ordinary, so unaware. A woman tugging a shopping trolley. A man on a bike, head down against the wind. The world didn't stop because someone disappeared. It never had.

But I couldn't shake the feeling that this wasn't just gossip. That there was something Marta hadn't said—or maybe didn't know how to. I typed her name into Instagram again. Still no updates. Her last post was six months ago, then nothing.

Something that stuck.

It was probably nothing. Probably.

But the hairs on my arms wouldn't lie flat for the rest of the lesson.

Chapter 6

I hadn't realized how long I'd been staring into space, my thoughts tangled and far from the little table in front of me. The soft clatter of cups and quiet conversation barely registered, until a shadow fell across the table, and a voice broke through the haze.

"Would you like anything else, Mademoiselle?" the waiter enquired, his figure casting a long shadow over me like an imposing silhouette.

I shook my head, my eyes darting around the bustling café with a sense of nervousness. The sun was at its zenith, casting a warm glow through the large windows, and I suddenly realised I'd been seated for an entire hour, adrift in my own thoughts. The waiter's silent insistence for me to vacate the table hung in the air like a tangible weight, yet I found myself anchored, unable to rise. Just then, my phone burst into a sharp, jarring ring, the screen flashing with a private number.

"Hello," I answered, my voice barely steady, laced with unease.

For a beat, there was only silence, a thick, unnatural pause that seemed to choke the air itself. The world held its breath.

Then came the voice.

"Bonjour, Laura."

It cut through the stillness like a blade, smooth yet charged with something dark — a sickly blend of false warmth and quiet threat. I didn't recognize it, but something deep inside me recoiled. My instincts flared like sirens. This wasn't a stranger. This was a predator.

Panic erupted inside me, a monstrous tidal wave crashing down with relentless force, as my eyes darted frantically across the bustling café. Each face transformed into a potential menace; the barista with a friendly smile appeared to harbour hidden malice, and even the woman in the corner, tenderly feeding her child, seemed wrapped in a sinister shadow. The clinking of cups and murmured conversations blurred into a dissonant hum, heightening the oppressive atmosphere that pressed in from all sides.

"What do you want?" The words stumbled out of my mouth, my heart pounding like a war drum, ferociously demanding answers yet dreading the terrifying truth that lurked just beyond the edge of revelation.

"You should make it easy for yourself. This running is futile. Don't bother with the police; they'll dismiss you, especially after you've squandered their time." The call cut abruptly, leaving me with a knot of fear.

My phone's battery was dwindling down to a mere thirty percent, the screen dimmer with each passing moment. Panic surged through me like a wave, urgency clawing at my mind as I stood to leave the cozy café, its warm lights casting a comforting glow over the polished wooden tables. Yet, a part of me wanted to stay, to bask a little longer in the calm before the chaos outside.

"Excuse me, Mademoiselle," a voice suddenly pierced the air, each syllable a sharp jolt to my frazzled nerves. Was the caller, the one I'd been evading, here among the shadows, waiting to expose me? But it was only the waiter, his presence benign yet startling.

"Your bill," he said, his words cutting cleanly through the fog of my paranoia, reminding me of the simple reality before me. A reality I both wanted to escape and stay rooted in.

Realizing in my haste I had forgotten to pay for my coffee, I fumbled with my wallet, tossing ten euros onto the table with a trembling hand. I avoided meeting his eyes, their potential curiosity too much to bear, and hurried out, the café door swinging shut behind me with a soft chime.

I knew exactly where I needed to go next, the destination clears in my mind, yet a part of me hesitated. Dread coiled tightly within my chest. The last thing I wanted was to drag them into the swirling vortex of danger that surrounded me, a storm I wished to weather alone. But the need for support, for someone to share the burden, tugged me just as fiercely.

Chapter 7

The door of the suburban house on that quiet, tree-lined street swung open the moment I rang the bell, revealing a warm glow from within. "Laura, what a surprise! What brings you here?" Aoife exclaimed, her face a tapestry of delight and confusion. Her eyes sparkled with curiosity, and her lips curved into a welcoming smile, even as her brows knit together in puzzled interest.

Our initial encounter unfolded at the charming Irish Club, a cozy haven nestled within the European Commission building on Rue Le Titien. The venue was a delightful blend of elegance and comfort, adorned with rich wooden accents that exuded warmth, creating an inviting atmosphere. The club hosted a lively meet-and-greet for international au pairs on the first Sunday of every month, a tradition that brought together individuals from all corners of the globe. The air was abuzz with a delightful mix of laughter and diverse languages, weaving a symphony of cultural exchange that was both intoxicating and heartwarming. I believed it would be an excellent opportunity to forge connections with others navigating similar paths, all gathered under the soft glow of hanging lanterns. These lanterns cast a gentle, golden light that danced across the room, illuminating eager faces ready to share their stories and experiences.

My very first au pair club meeting took place on a bright Sunday morning, a day when most nannies enjoyed a rare respite from their duties. As I stepped into the gathering, I was greeted with warmth by one of the organisers. "Hi, I'm Charlotte, I haven't seen you around before," she announced with a friendly, welcoming smile that instantly put me at ease. Charlotte seemed to be in her early twenties, radiating a vibrant energy that was perfectly matched by her stylish and chic appearance.

She wore a pair of well-fitted jeans that hugged her form gracefully, paired with a printed top that added a lively splash of colour to her ensemble. Her sleek black boots clicked softly on the floor as she moved, completing her look with a touch of elegance. Her hair was styled impeccably, each strand in place as if guided by an invisible hand, and her makeup was applied with meticulous precision. It highlighted her natural features beautifully, lending her an aura of polished confidence that was both inspiring and approachable.

"You must be new to the nanny world," she said with a warm smile, her eyes sparkling with friendliness. "It's simple, really. Just sign in here with your full name, your suburb, and your mobile number. " She pointed to a neatly arranged sign-in sheet, its lines ready to capture the details of newcomers. The room was inviting, sunlight streaming through the large window and casting a gentle glow on the area set up for refreshments. A small table was adorned with a charming array of tea, coffee, and chilled beverages, their inviting aromas mingling in the air. "It makes it easier for everyone to organise meetups," she continued, "and we even have a Facebook page you can join," her voice laced with enthusiasm as she gestured towards the inviting space, encouraging a sense of community and connection.

I first noticed Aoife as she stood amidst a lively circle of girls, her voice animatedly filling the air with stories about her host family. She wasn't the stereotypical image of an Irish girl with blonde locks and flashy jewellery; instead, her charm radiated from a captivating smile that seemed capable of winning over anyone in her vicinity.

"My family is just wonderful," she exclaimed with a hint of pride, her eyes sparkling with genuine affection. "They treat me amazingly well. I even get to use their car, and I have an entire room downstairs all to myself," she continued, her words painting a vivid picture of her fortunate circumstances.

The expressions on some of the girls' faces revealed a mix of admiration and envy as they listened to her recount the many perks of her position, each detail more enticing than the last.

The memory faded as I shifted my weight on the front step, the present moment rushing back in with the scent of jasmine and the creak of Aoife's door.

"Surprise, I thought I'd drop by. Sorry if I caught you in the middle of something; I should have called ahead," I said, glancing around the room filled with the warm glow of afternoon sunlight streaming through the windows.

"What are you doing here? Apologies if that sounded weird," Aoife responded, her eyes widening in surprise before her expression softened into a welcoming smile. "I wasn't expecting you, but it's fine. The family I work for loves having visitors," she joked, gesturing towards the inviting interior. "Come in, would you like something to drink?" she asked, her voice friendly and inviting.

"No, thanks, I'm alright," I replied, waving off the offer politely while taking in the homely ambiance, the faint aroma of fresh flowers mingling with the scent of brewing coffee.

"Sebastian's fast asleep, and Lucas is busily engrossed in playing in his room, so it's the perfect time for my clandestine cigarette break," she said with a conspiratorial wink, guiding me out to the sun-dappled back patio. The air was cool and crisp, carrying the faint scent of blooming jasmine from the garden.

"Aren't you supposed to be working today?" she asked, raising an eyebrow.

"No, plans shifted unexpectedly at the last minute with the kids. Camille swooped in and picked them up, whisking them off to a friend's place for the evening, so I suddenly found myself with a rare pocket of free time," I explained, enjoying the unexpected respite.

"I always thought the French were a regimented bunch, always sticking to their schedules," she chuckled, her laughter mingling with the rustle of leaves in the gentle breeze.

"Those are the Germans," I replied, grinning as the sun began to dip lower in the sky, painting the horizon with hues of amber and rose.

We engaged in light, breezy conversation, touching on inconsequential topics for a while. Aoife, surrounded by a host of admirers, animatedly recounted stories of the attention she often attracted. Her eyes sparkled with amusement as she spoke, and I couldn't help but smile at the sight of her effortless charm and flirtation—an art she mastered with ease, in contrast to my own awkward attempts.

After a moment, I hesitated, my mind battling between pride and necessity, before finally asking, "Could I possibly borrow some cash? I promise I'll pay you back." A wave of embarrassment washed over me as I made the request, yet I found myself with no other choice.

"Sure, but is everything okay?" she asked, her face a canvas of genuine concern and curiosity, her eyebrows slightly furrowed and eyes wide, making me question if I should have asked at all.

"Yeah, I just lost my purse and don't get paid until the end of the week," I explained, my voice carrying a hint of frustration. "I really don't want to burden my host family—they wouldn't think fondly of it. I completely understand if you can't help."

"No, it's alright. How much do you need?" she replied, her hand gracefully reaching for her bag, the soft leather rustling as she did so.

"Three hundred euros, if you can spare that," I said, my voice steady yet hopeful.

"I'll call you later, okay?" I assured her as I left, my mind racing with determination not to endanger either her or the kids in any way.

"Is everything alright, Laura? You seem a little off," she called after me, her voice tinged with worry, echoing softly in the cool evening air.

"No, I'm just tired. I'm going to head back and get an early night," I responded, attempting a reassuring smile.

"Alright, well call me if you need anything else," she shouted from the doorstep, her voice carrying warmth and sincerity.

"I will, and thanks again," I said, my gratitude palpable as I closed the gate behind me, the latch clicking softly in the stillness of the night.

Chapter 8

Each Sunday Camille graciously granted me a day off from work, and I always seized the opportunity to make the most of it. On this particular day, I set my sights on exploring the vibrant city of Cologne, nestled just over the border in Germany. The journey was a bit lengthy, a two-hour train ride that unfolded like a scenic tapestry through rolling hills and picturesque villages, with fields of wildflowers swaying gently in the breeze and quaint cottages dotting the landscape, making it a full day's adventure. As I stepped off the train and set foot in Cologne, my senses were immediately ensnared by the majestic beauty of its cathedral. This towering structure, an architectural marvel recognised as a world heritage site, soared into the sky with its gothic spires piercing the clouds. Each spire reached for the heavens, intricate and detailed, like finely chiselled sculptures. Its imposing presence cast an enchanting shadow over the city, exuding a domineering aura that left me utterly spellbound. The intricate stonework, a mosaic of finely carved figures and ornate designs, seemed alive with history. The stained-glass windows, glowing in the sunlight, splashed vivid colours across the cathedral's interior, creating a kaleidoscope of light that danced on the ancient stone floors. It was one of the most breathtaking edifices I had ever laid eyes on, a true testament to human artistry and devotion, each element whispering tales of centuries past.

By the time I returned to the house, the clock hands had nearly reached eleven o'clock at night. As I navigated my way back along the silent, dimly lit streets, the world seemed hushed and still, with only the occasional rustle of leaves or distant bark of a dog breaking the tranquillity. I was acutely aware of the need to tread softly, the soles of my shoes barely brushing the cobblestones, so as not to disturb the peaceful slumber of those nestled comfortably in their homes.

However, as I turned the corner onto Rue Du Couloir, the familiar street name etched into the stone wall, I was taken aback stood a man I hadn't yet met but instantly recognised from the family photos in the lounge — Pierre. He was deep in conversation with a shadowy figure, their faces partially obscured by the warm flicker of the streetlamp outside. My breath caught as I stepped back, instinctively pressing into the wall. I wasn't supposed to see this. The ease in Pierre's posture, the hushed intensity of the exchange — it all felt... off. As if I'd stumbled into a moment not meant for me. The day had already been full of unease, and now the night, it seemed, had its own secrets to whisper. The unexpected sight, lit by the golden glow of the streetlamp, caught me off guard, adding an intriguing twist to the end of my already eventful day, as if the night itself held a secret yet to be revealed.

"Where did you put it?" Pierre's voice sliced through the cacophony of the quiet street, his finger jabbing like a dagger at a shadowy figure concealed beneath the folds of a long trench coat and the brim of a tilted hat. The presence of this enigmatic figure exuded an almost palpable aura of danger, a stark contrast to the type of company I ever imagined Pierre keeping.

"You don't have to worry," the man replied with a chilling nonchalance, releasing a thick plume of cigarette smoke that twisted through the air like a spectral serpent. His voice was steady, almost unnervingly so, as if each word had been drilled into him through countless repetitions, a sinister mantra echoing through the air.

Before I could slip away unnoticed, Pierre's head turned sharply in my direction—as though he'd sensed me the moment I rounded the corner. His gaze locked onto mine with unnerving precision, and a broad smile unfurled across his face. It was warm, effortless—too effortless. The kind of smile meant to disarm, to suggest everything was perfectly ordinary. His smile was polished, but it didn't reach his eyes. 'You ask a lot of questions, Laura,' he said. 'Curiosity can be dangerous.'

But it wasn't.

It was too late to hide.

I walked slowly toward the house, each step deliberate, my boots brushing against the stone path with a soft, rhythmic scrape. The air was still. Heavy. Pierre stood just outside the front door, posture casual—one hand tucked into his coat pocket, the other resting against the doorframe like he had all the time in the world.

Beside him stood a man I didn't recognize. He didn't turn to look at me, but the set of his shoulders shifted, a slight angle adjusting as if to register my approach without offering the courtesy of acknowledgement. That subtle movement alone sent a chill through me.

As I drew closer, he stepped away from Pierre without a word and descended the stone steps, slow and purposeful. His footsteps made no sound—only the growing presence of him marked the space between us. He was tall—well over six feet—and built like someone accustomed to strength, not show. His head was shaved close, his face angular and pale, with sharp, unflinching features that made no attempt to soften. His pale blue eyes locked onto mine, and I felt the full weight of them—measured, assessing, and without a trace of warmth.

There was no nod. No greeting. Just a calculated pause as he passed me, his stare brushing over me like a blade, leaving a line of cold in its wake.

Then he was gone—swallowed by the edge of the street like he'd never been there at all.

I reached the base of the steps, pulse thudding low in my throat.

Pierre hadn't moved. His smile remained perfectly in place, as if nothing unsettling had just occurred. His smile was polished, but it didn't reach his eyes. 'You ask a lot of questions, Laura,' he said. 'Curiosity can be dangerous.'

"Bonsoir, Laura," he said smoothly. "Did you have a nice day out?"

"Hi," I responded, sensing the lingering warmth of the day caressing my skin like a gentle embrace. I added with a smile, "Yes, it was good. I'm becoming more and more familiar with my surroundings with each passing day."

I pressed on into the house where Pierre awaited ominously in the doorway. As I slipped past him, the door swung shut behind us with a soft yet final thud, sealing us away from the biting chill of the night. "I wasn't expecting you to be up this late, I'm sorry that I disturbed you both" I remarked, the hushed intimacy of our secluded space a stark contrast to the earlier charged encounter.

Pierre's voice was brisk and unapologetic. "Yes, I have an early trip to Paris in the morning, and there are a few things I must sort out before I go. If you'll excuse me, I need to retrieve something from my office."

Leaving Pierre to his task, I meandered into the kitchen, where the gentle hum of the refrigerator filled the air with a cool, inviting glow. As I opened the fridge and retrieved a glass of water, the refreshing coldness tingled against my fingers, and I planned to take it upstairs to quench my thirst. That's when my attention was caught by Pierre's laptop, left slightly ajar on the sleek, granite countertop. The screen glowed softly, displaying details about a man named **Harold Kemp**—an unfamiliar name that nonetheless piqued my curiosity. The photograph of Kemp portrayed a man in his mid to late thirties, exuding a rugged Mediterranean allure, with eyes that seemed to harbour secrets yet untold. His brief biography revealed him as the head of the security division at a company called Delta Inc., a role he had diligently held for nearly a decade.

"Can I help you with something, Laura?" Pierre's voice cut through the stillness of the kitchen, startling me as he abruptly snapped the laptop lid shut. The sharp click resonated in the quiet room, magnifying the tension.

"Oh, no, sorry—I didn't mean to look. My apologies," I stammered, my cheeks burning with a sudden rush of guilt, feeling as though I had intruded on something private and forbidden.

"Bonne nuit," Pierre interjected, his tone cold and final, leaving little room for further discussion. It was a subtle yet firm command, suggesting that it was time for me to retreat for the evening.

"Good night." I echoed softly, my voice barely above a whisper as I turned and made my way up the stairs to my bedroom. With each step, a chill of unease crept over me, a disquieting, silent warning that lingered in the air. Something in his stern gaze, in the secrets that seemed to hover just out of reach, whispered that all was not as it seemed.

Chapter 9

The following Tuesday, as normal I made my way to my French class at the Alliance Francaise school, conveniently nestled on Avenue des Arts. As I stepped inside, a flutter of anxiety washed over me at the thought of speaking only in French, aware that my skills were still quite rudimentary. However, I quickly found solace in the realisation that everyone else shared the same level of proficiency. Camille, in her wisdom, had enrolled me in the beginners' class, which turned out to be the perfect fit.

The classroom was hosting no more than ten people, each bringing their own unique story and background. We hailed from diverse countries and walks of life. Some were spouses of EU employees, drawn to Brussels by their partner's work, while others were military personnel stationed at the large US base nearby. Among us was a Chinese woman, adding to the rich tapestry of our group. There were also individuals like me, fortunate enough to have employers who covered the cost of the lessons, making this linguistic journey possible.

The hour-long lesson seemed to fly by in the blink of an eye, and before I knew it, the time had come to pack up and leave. A part of me fervently hoped that the tutor wouldn't call on me to speak in French, fully aware of how clumsy and awkward my pronunciation was. Yet, at the same time, an insatiable curiosity and a yearning to delve deeper into the language tugged at my heart, compelling me to want to learn more despite my apprehensions.

As class wrapped up, I gathered my things slowly, the room around me dissolving into the usual hum of closing notebooks and casual goodbyes. Madame Ricard called out a cheerful "À demain!" as she wiped the whiteboard clean.

I slipped my tote bag over my shoulder and followed the small stream of students out into the narrow hallway that led toward reception. A noticeboard near the entrance caught my eye—paper corners flapping lightly in the draft from the main doors. I almost walked past it. Almost.

But something about the white sheet tacked dead-centre on the board made me pause.

MISSING

The word was printed in bold, block letters at the top, just above a photo of a girl smiling wide for the camera, sunlight catching the edge of her dark-blonde hair. Her name was written below in simple type:

Erin Blake, Age 22
Canadian National – Last seen in Brussels, March 14
If you have any information, please contact local authorities or the
Canadian Embassy.

My breath caught slightly as I stepped closer.

There was something deeply unnerving about seeing her face printed like that—caught forever in some past, carefree moment. I recognized her immediately. It was the same girl Marie had mentioned earlier in class. The one who'd just... vanished.

I studied the picture for a moment. She was pretty. Friendly-looking. Not much older than me. She wore a denim jacket over a sundress, standing in what looked like Parc du Cinquantenaire. There was even a waffle in her hand, half-eaten, like she'd been mid-laugh when someone took the photo.

Below her photo, smaller tear-off slips had already been taken—probably by students or teachers trying to be helpful. But what could they really do?

I felt a strange chill snake through my spine.

She had come to Brussels for an experience, like I had. Worked as an au pair, like I did. We walked these same corridors, maybe even sat in the classroom next door.

And now her smile was pinned to a board under the word Missing.

"How's life treating you in Brussels, Laura?" Sonia, my Spanish classmate, with her warm, inviting smile and a slight accent that always reminded me of sunlit beaches, enquired as we lingered in the bustling school's lobby after class. The air was filled with the chatter of students and the faint scent of coffee, while the afternoon sunlight streamed through the large windows, casting soft shadows across the polished floor.

"It's going well for now," I replied, though my words lacked conviction as my attention drifted to the television behind the reception desk. The screen was ablaze with the urgent, pulsating glow of a breaking news alert, casting an eerie light across the room. The haunting image flickered repeatedly, each flash revealing the same man I'd seen under the dim glow of Pierre's laptop the previous Sunday evening. His face was etched with a certain severity, the lines deep and shadowed, while his eyes seemed to pierce through the screen, holding secrets that begged to be uncovered. His expression was both enigmatic and intense, as if he carried the weight of untold stories within his gaze.

"Harold Kemp was discovered dead in his apartment by his partner this morning," the news anchor declared, her voice cutting through the room sharply. Despite my poor grasp of French, I recognised the word "MORT". The news anchor switched to a live report from outside the building, where police officers stood by as the body, draped with a blanket, was being taken away. The reporter went on to say, "Harold Kemp worked as a senior analyst at Delta Inc., one of the leading data companies in Brussels."

"Sonia, what happened to that guy on the TV?" I demanded with urgency, my voice taut with tension as it coiled and tightened.

"Que?" she shot back, her voice sharp with surprise as she tore her eyes away from the dense pages of her textbooks. Her gaze shifted to the television screen, the flickering light casting shadows on her focused expression. As she began to relay the presenter's grave announcement, her words carried the weight of the news, her tone a mix of disbelief and urgency.

"His partner discovered him unresponsive after a few days without a word. Authorities report he was found in bed, seemingly having slipped away peacefully in his sleep. Mr. Kemp had only just been elevated to a senior position in the company," she continued, her words pounding like a relentless drumbeat, each sentence heavy with the weight of unexpected loss.

"Do you know him?" she enquired softly, her fingers resting lightly on my shoulder, a gentle connection that conveyed both curiosity and reassurance.

"No, not really, just curious," I lied, my voice carrying a casual tone that belied the slight unease I felt inside.

"It's all anyone can talk about, and it's just around the block from here, he must have had a heart attack!" Sonia exclaimed, her eyes wide with a mixture of intrigue and disbelief that bordered on frantic excitement.

"I guess so," I murmured, staring at the screen, mind reeling. Kemp. Dead. The name and face circled in my chest, a relentless reminder. Was it the threat? Was it meant for me?

We stepped outside, the city buzzing with its usual hum of traffic and life. The winter air was crisp, biting against my cheeks, but I barely noticed as my thoughts spiraled. Sonia chatted about her weekend plans, her words a blur against the roaring in my ears.

"See you next week, Laura!" she called, waving as she headed toward her car.

"See you," I replied, distracted.

I turned toward the tram stop, footsteps quickening. Camille's voice echoed in my mind. Her urgency. Did she know something like this would happen? With every glance around, paranoia tightened its grip.

Chapter 10

I jolted awake, my heart pounding like a war drum, my breaths ragged and shallow. As my eyes flitted across the unfamiliar room, a wave of disorientation crashed over me, relentless and consuming. For a moment, I was adrift, unsure where I was or why. But then, in a tumultuous rush, reality struck; I was in the modest hotel room I'd booked, using Aoife's money, near the frenetic heartbeat of the Gare du Nord train station. Memories of the previous night collided with my consciousness; I'd spent eighty euros on this bare-bones refuge. I felt torn between relief for having a place to stay and guilt for spending so much of Aoife's money.

The room was a study in simplicity: a narrow twin bed, its frame creaking slightly under the weight of a thin, slightly worn duvet. The fabric was faded, with a pattern that had once been vibrant but was now muted by time. The bathroom was small, with tiles that bore the marks of years gone by, each crack and chip a testament to time's relentless march. A small balcony, barely large enough for a chair, jutted out from the room, offering a modest view of a tranquil side street below. The street was lined with trees whose leaves rustled softly in a gentle breeze, a quiet reminder that this was not the Ritz.

The previous night, I had gathered just enough loose change to purchase a cheap second-hand charger and added some credit to my phone. As I scrolled through the clutter of my messages, a missed call from Aoife stood out like a beacon in the chaos. Her text message followed, imbued with the comforting warmth of her familiar tone:

Hi, I've finished work for the day, so I thought I'd give you a call. Call me back when you get this.

The words wrapped around me like a warm blanket on a

chilly evening. I quickly composed a reply, my fingers dancing nervously over the screen as I tried to mask my anxiety with a flimsy excuse about having forgotten to charge my phone overnight.

Despite my overwhelming reluctance, the realisation hit me like a storm, leaving me feeling trapped. I had no choice but to return to my host family's house. My passport, that vital document, was safely stored in my room with all my other belongings. It always resided in the main compartment of my small, well-worn backpack, ready for any adventure that might beckon. Yet, the thought of going back there filled me with dread, twisting my stomach into uneasy knots. It was an unavoidable detour if I ever hoped to leave the confines of Brussels, yet every step back felt like a betrayal of my desire to move forward.

Driven by an intense yearning to regain some semblance of dignity and constrained by a tight budget, I made my way to a thrift store, hoping to find second-hand clothing that would suit my needs. The store was a treasure trove of forgotten garments, each with its own story. After sifting through racks of clothes, I settled on a grey hoodie and a pair of well-worn jeans. The hoodie, with its slightly frayed cuffs and soft, worn fabric, offered a reassuring warmth against the chill of my worries. It felt like a familiar embrace, gentle and comforting. The jeans, faded but sturdy, seemed to promise resilience. Afterward, I visited a nearby supermarket to pick up some toiletries. The fresh, invigorating scent of soap and shampoo suggested a new beginning, a subtle whisper of renewal as I stepped out onto the bustling street.

As I walked towards my employer's residence in the picturesque yet intimidating neighbourhood of Ixelles, each step felt laden with an almost palpable weight, as though my very soul was dragging the ground. The cobblestone footpaths, meticulously arranged with a precision that spoke of centuries of care, were flanked by charming townhouses, each boasting ornate facades adorned with intricate carvings and wrought-iron embellishments. Leafy trees, their branches swaying gently in the soft breeze, whispering secrets of old, their rustling leaves creating an ambient symphony that mingled with the rhythmic echo of my footfalls against the stones. This heaviness was a peculiar blend of hesitation and urgency, a physical manifestation of the intense inner turmoil swirling within me. Emotions like fear, hope, and shame clashed violently, creating a chaotic whirlwind of feelings in my mind, much like a storm brewing on a silent night. Dark clouds gathered ominously overhead, casting long shadows that danced across the ground. The air was thick with anticipation, a palpable tension that seemed to coil around me, and every shadow seemed to deepen the sense of conflict within me, as if the very atmosphere conspired to mirror the tempest raging in my heart.

Chapter 11

I fell in love with Brussels, a city bursting with vibrant energy, where friendly locals welcome you with warm smiles and a myriad of cultures blend seamlessly together. During my brief stay, I fully immersed myself in its rich tapestry of offerings and formed cherished friendships along the way. On Friday nights, when I wasn't babysitting, I often spent time with Aoife, who had quickly become a close friend. Together, we frequently ventured to the numerous eateries along the bustling Rue des Bouchers. This lively pedestrian street was a visual and olfactory delight, lined with tables draped in vibrant, colourful cloths and adorned with chalkboard menus displaying tantalising dishes. The air was thick with the mouthwatering aromas of global cuisines, featuring everything from the savory spices of Spanish paella, with its saffron-infused rice and fresh seafood, to the hearty and robust flavours of Argentinian dishes, rich with grilled meats and chimichurri sauce.

Our culinary explorations often led us to sample various cuisines, and for this evening's escapade, we had chosen a quaint, traditional Flemish eatery named Le Mormiton. Conscious of our limited budget, we opted to share an abundant serving of mussels bathed in a rich white wine sauce. The dish was complemented by tender boiled potatoes and slices of crusty, golden-brown bread that crackled under our fingers. To accompany our meal, we selected the most affordable bottle of wine or beer available on the menu, eager to savour every last drop of this modest yet satisfying feast.

Later that evening, we made our way to a bar called Le Cercueil on Rue des Harengs, which Aoife had suggested. It was famous for its perfect blend of beers and live bands playing all types of music.

"What would you like to drink, Aoife?" I asked as I leaned over the shiny wooden bar, illuminated by the soft lighting.

"Nothing for me, have you looked at these prices? Eleven euros for one drink?" she exclaimed, her eyes widening in shock as she checked the menu.

"Well, since we're already here," I replied, attempting to be reassuring. "Let's just have one drink and then move on to another place." Just then, the waitress came over to us, her face expressionless and unfriendly, as if she'd dealt with far too many patrons that day.

"Two Hoegaardens, please," I called out to her, my voice rising above the gentle hum of conversations and the rhythmic clinking of glasses that filled the dimly lit pub. The warm glow of the overhead lights cast a golden hue over the wooden tables and aged bar counter, creating an atmosphere of comfort and camaraderie.

Hoegaarden was a Belgian white beer that I cherished, even though it carried a robust strength that could catch one by surprise. Its cloudy, pale golden appearance was like a misty morning sun, hinting at the aromatic blend of coriander and orange peel that infused its flavour with a refreshing zest, while still delivering a potent punch. Each local beer was presented in a distinctive glass, crafted to highlight its unique qualities. The glass was a work of art, with its shape and weight complementing the beer's character, and its name elegantly emblazoned on the side in intricate lettering, ensuring that every sip was not just a drink but a celebration of its rich heritage and meticulous craftsmanship.

"I doubt we'll be able to find a table," I remarked, my eyes sweeping across the crowded room. The air buzzed with chatter and laughter, a cacophony of voices blending into a lively symphony. Every table seemed occupied, chairs filled with people animatedly gesturing and leaning in close to hear one another over the din. The warm glow of overhead lights reflected off polished wood surfaces, casting a nice but bustling atmosphere throughout the space.

"Try not to look, but those two guys are watching us," I whispered, a sly grin playing on my lips. The atmosphere was filled with light-hearted tension. "I told you not to look!" I exclaimed, a blend of disbelief and amusement in my voice as Aoife, unable to help herself, instantly turned her head to peek at them.

"They're not too bad, are they?" she laughed, her giggle a soft, melodious sound that seemed to dance through the air like a gentle breeze. Her laughter was light and airy, carrying with it an infectious joy that mingled seamlessly with the rustling leaves and the whisper of the wind, creating a harmonious symphony of nature and delight.

Enticed by the sound of our shared laughter, the two strangers started to weave their way through the bustling crowd. They moved with a deliberate grace, skillfully manoeuvring around clusters of people that dotted the lively scene. Each step they took seemed measured and purposeful, gradually closing the gap between us. As they drew nearer, their presence became increasingly perceptible, with their curious expressions glowing with eagerness, like moths drawn to the flicker of a flame.

"Good evening, ladies. May we join you?" the taller man enquired, his voice smooth and inviting.

"Not at all," I replied with a warm smile. "I'm Laura, and this is my friend Aoife." My eyes sparkled as I gestured to Aoife, who nodded in acknowledgment. "And you are?"

"I'm Joseph," he introduced himself with a courteous nod, "and this is Alex." The two men settled into the conversation easily. "What are your plans for the evening?" Joseph asked, his gaze resting on Aoife with genuine curiosity.

"We haven't decided yet," Aoife responded, her eyes twinkling with mischief as she took a sip of her drink, letting the cool liquid refresh her. "But the night is still young, so who knows what could happen!" Her playful smile hinted at the promise of adventure, and the air around their table buzzed with anticipation.

I could always rely on her to spark the conversation with her vivacious spirit, her words dancing through the air like fireflies on a summer night. As the evening wore on, Aoife's cheeks flushed a rosy hue, and her laughter bubbled up like effervescent champagne, filling the room with its infectious joy. Joseph, who insisted on being called Joe, was exceedingly generous, ensuring our glasses were never empty as he frequently ordered rounds of drinks with a broad, welcoming smile. I, on the other hand, opted to skip every second drink, choosing to savour the evening at a more relaxed and measured pace, letting each moment linger like a soothing melody. Alex, in contrast, was not much of a conversationalist; his quiet demeanour hung in the air, adding a slight tinge of awkwardness to our gathering, like a soft shadow cast by candlelight. Despite this, we managed to keep the small talk flowing, weaving together threads of conversation amidst the gentle hum and warm glow of the bustling bar.

Aoife began meeting Joseph weekly, and on occasion, Alex and I would join them, allowing me to become quite familiar with Alex. From what I understood about Aoife, she wasn't wholly committed to Joseph; she had a few other suitors in her life. Aoife always liked to keep her options open, embodying a playful spirit that reflected her easy-going approach to relationships. Her mischievous charm was evident in the way her eyes danced with laughter, hinting at secrets she held close, and in her casual shrug whenever topics of commitment arose.

Chapter 12

"Alex, what are you doing here?" I asked, gripping the cold metal handrail as I steadied myself on the daycare's broad concrete steps.

A cluster of toddlers tumbled out ahead of me, their laughter echoing off the brightly painted walls. I'd just dropped Camille's two little ones off—Camille had sprinted out at dawn for an early shift—when I nearly ran into him.

He brushed a lock of dark hair from his forehead and offered a lopsided grin. "Hi. I was passing through on business. I thought you lived over in Ixelles?"

The sky was that washed-out blue early morning as I took in his crisp navy blazer and slim trousers, impeccably pressed despite whatever whirlwind conference he'd emerged from. "I do," I said, returning his smile. "But I just dropped the kids off at daycare. Now I'm headed home to tackle some laundry."

Alex's eyes lit up. "Got time for a quick coffee? There's a little café just across the street—wooden tables, the smell of fresh pastries. Thought it might be a good spot to chat."

I glanced at my phone: 8:15. The sidewalks were only just waking up, a few bleary commuters ambling by. Thirty minutes wasn't much, but it was enough. "Sure," I said. "I've got half an hour to burn."

We crossed the narrow Rue de la Crèche, the pavement mosaic glinting with tiny stones. The café's facade was simple, large paned windows smudged with dew, a tiny chalkboard advertising "Today's Fresh Bake". Inside, the afternoon sunlight streamed over polished oak tables. A low hum of quiet conversation mingled with the hiss of the espresso machine.

We settled into two rattan chairs by the window. The waiter—

tall, with a neatly trimmed beard—brought over two steaming mugs in under a minute. The coffee's rich aroma rose in golden tendrils between us. I inhaled deeply before lifting my cup.

Alex leaned back, folding one leg over the other. "It's nice to talk somewhere other than the office bar," he said, swirling his dark roast. "So, how's family life?"

I let the question roll against the warmth of my coffee. Outside, a delivery truck rumbled past, and the café's door chimed.

"Different," I replied. "They're lovely people, but I don't really know them that well. They guard their privacy; I'm the nanny, so I only see what they let me see." I traced a drop of cream on my mug's rim. "That's fine by me. It's just a job, and I don't expect us to be more than colleagues. I'm not on their invitation list for dinners or weekend barbecues, so I rarely meet their friends or co-workers."

Alex studied me over the rim of his cup. I could see genuine curiosity in his dark eyes. He set his mug down and fished a glossy business card from his jacket pocket:

"Project Manager—Longreach Logistics" it read in crisp lettering.

"Burying myself in meetings and client pitches lately," he said, handing it to me. "It's hectic, but I like the pace."

I turned the card between my fingers, the paper cool and weighty. "Project manager, huh? It has a nice ring to it. Suits you." I offered him a small, approving smile.

I'd always known he worked in a marketing ad firm that specialised in social media campaigns—but I hadn't seen him in full business regalia before. His tailored suit fit him like it was made just for his frame: broad shoulders, slim waist. He looked at ease; in that moment, I realised I found him even more attractive than before.

A glance at my phone brought me back to reality: 8:40 a.m. I stood, smoothing the front of my cardigan. "Oh! I should get going, I've a lot to do today before I pick them up." On autopilot, I gave him the customary two light kisses on the cheeks—la bise —then waved as I stepped back onto the sidewalk.

I slipped Alex's card into my bag as he shouted, "Catch you on the weekend, right?"

I glanced over my shoulder. "Definitely," I said, and then turned toward the metro station, my shoes clicking against the mosaic as I hurried back. I boarded Line 1 at Montgomery, the map etched into my memory now from survival rather than sightseeing.

The metro station was quiet, the morning rush easing into a lull. I took a seat by the window and watched the city glide past— narrow brick houses, tram wires crisscrossing the sky, a blur of cyclists. I boarded Line 1 at Montgomery, the map etched into my memory now from survival rather than sightseeing.

Alex's business card sat in the side pocket of my bag, forgotten until I brushed against it. It felt oddly formal, unnecessary. Still, I left it there.

Back at the house, sunlight spilled through the tall windows, warming the stone floors and lighting up the floating dust in Camille's perfectly organised entryway. I kicked off my boots and padded toward the kitchen, enjoying the silence. It was rare, and I'd learned to savour it.

Laundry. Lunch prep. A quick tidying of the playroom. My day folded into familiar routines. I moved on instinct, grateful for the rhythm.

But when I passed the study, I stopped.

The door, usually left ajar, was closed.

Not locked. Not strange, exactly. Just... closed.

I paused for half a second, waiting for a sound. Nothing. I kept walking. No need to overthink it.

By noon, I'd made a dent in the laundry pile and even managed to sit with a cup of tea at the dining table. I scrolled the news. Still more about Kemp—updates from investigators, speculation from journalists, photos I hadn't seen before.

One image showed him standing in front of a government building, his expression unreadable. Another was taken at a conference. A third, cropped and grainy, showed him talking to someone just out of frame. The caption said: "Unidentified associate." I leaned closer, my pulse skipping. The silhouette beside Kemp was familiar. Broad shoulders, a dark coat. The photo was blurry, but something about it looked like Pierre.

I stared at it for a moment too long.

Then my phone rang—Camille.

"Can you pick the kids up early today?" she asked. Her voice was brisk but steady. "I've got back-to-back meetings. I won't make it on time."

"Of course. Everything okay?"

A brief pause. "Yes. Just—let's keep things calm for the rest of the day, alright?"

"Sure."

"Merci."

She hung up without waiting for a goodbye.

By one-thirty, I was back at the daycare gate, the low winter sun casting long shadows across the courtyard. The air had cooled since morning, crisp against my cheeks. A bell chimed faintly from inside, and moments later Max came barreling out of the building, his backpack askew and arms overflowing with crumpled, half-finished drawings. His eyes lit up when he saw me.

"Regarde ce que j'ai fait!" he shouted, nearly colliding with my legs as he held up a red-and-green blur that might've been a dragon, who knew. I laughed, steadying him with one arm while smoothing the edge of his jacket.

Chloe was waiting downstairs in the crèche, sitting patiently beside the assistant on a tiny chair that barely held her. She looked up at me with wide eyes, her thumb in her mouth. I crouched down to fix the strap of her shoe, which had come loose, then scooped up her bag and reached for Max's hand.

"Ready?" I asked, and both nodded.

We stepped out into the quiet side street, the pavement damp and glinting from a recent drizzle. As we rounded the corner onto Rue de la Crèche, something flickered at the edge of my vision—movement across the road. A figure, quick and deliberate, slipped into the driver's seat of a dark car parked just beyond the school's rear gate. The door shut with a dull thud, followed by the low growl of the engine turning over. It didn't pull away. It just sat there. Idling.

I slowed, then glanced again. The windows were tinted, the kind that turned glass into mirrors. I couldn't see the driver's face. Could've been another parent. Could've been anyone.

Still, the hairs on the back of my neck rose.

I tightened my grip on Max's hand and shifted Chloe closer against my side. She clutched my coat with her small fingers, pressing in as we continued walking—faster now, not running, but enough to put distance between us and that idling car.

Just in case.

"Can we get a pain au chocolat?" Max asked, obliviously.

"Maybe later," I said, eyes flicking back to the street behind us.

Whoever it was, they didn't follow.

But the feeling stayed with me.

Like something was shifting. Quietly. Just out of view.

Chapter 13

Ixelles was a lovely part of Brussels. It had beautiful, cobbled streets which made it a very distinctive neighbourhood along with lots of cafés and restaurants that always seemed to be busy, and you could easily pass the day in. The area consisted mainly of townhouses which were three to four storeys in height.

It had been nearly a week since I last stood on this doorstep, but the house looked exactly the same.

Number fourteen on Rue du Couloir—quiet, composed, indifferent. The ivy still curled up the railing. The same crack split the corner of the step. But as I stood there now, everything felt different. Heavier.

Reality settled around me like a weighted coat.

No footsteps. No voices. Just silence.

The sound echoed in the stillness, and I quickly darted to the corner of the street to observe if anyone would respond. The seconds stretched, and to my relief, the door remained unanswered. With cautious steps, I crossed the narrow street, retrieved the cold metal key from my pocket, and quietly turned the lock. The door creaked open, and I stepped inside.

The house wrapped around me in an unsettling silence, a jarring contrast to the usual lively clamour of children playing that once filled the air with laughter and shouts. The absence of sound was disconcerting, almost as if the very walls were holding their breath, waiting for something to break the stillness. I bypassed the living room entirely; its familiar furniture now seemed ghostly and faded in my memory, like relics from a bygone era. I headed straight for the staircase, its wooden steps creaking softly underfoot, leading me upwards. My destination was my attic bedroom, a secluded haven at the top of the house, where the slanted ceilings and dusty beams provided a comforting embrace.

I reached for the metal cord, its chill biting into my palm like winter's breath, and tugged it down to reveal the creaking, retractable staircase. Each step I took felt heavier as I ascended, a growing sense of unease curling around me like a dense, invisible fog. Upon reaching the attic, my heart skipped a beat at the sight before me: the room was utterly desolate. Where once there had been signs of life, now there was nothing. The bed, the wardrobe, every trace of my existence had vanished as if swept away by an unseen hand. The walls stood naked, stripped of memories, with only the faded outlines of where pictures once hung to suggest any history. The only thing there was my backpack, which I had left casually draped over the arm of a chair; it was empty, but I took it anyway. It was as though I had never lived there, as if no soul had occupied this space for an eternity, leaving behind only the silence of abandonment.

As I descended the stairs, a sudden, violent creak from the front door exploded through the silence, sending a surge of terror searing through my veins and freezing me in place. My mind whirled in a panic-stricken frenzy, paralysed by an overwhelming fear, my instincts screaming for escape but unable to decide where to run. In a desperate heartbeat, I hurled myself into Camille's bedroom, my ear pressed frantically against the door, while my heart thundered in my chest like a war drum. Muffled voices rose menacingly from the ground floor, a cacophony of indistinct and eerie shadows, but undeniably male—a stranger's voice, a sinister murmur into his mobile. Driven by an insatiable, burning compulsion to unmask the intruder, I cautiously inched the bedroom door open and crept to the top of the stairs, each step a treacherous gamble. There he stood—the very man who had exchanged words with Pierre at the front door. A bone-chilling question gripped me with icy fingers: what was he doing inside the house, and how had he obtained a key? My fingers fumbled. I wasn't trained for this reason. I was improvising with every breath.

"You have a reservation on the 5:20 train from Paris to Brussels tonight. Be at Midi Station by five o'clock sharp. I've just found her passport and bank cards where you said you put them, she's cornered now, trust me. It baffles me how she's managed to slip through our fingers for so long. But not anymore. See you then," he said, his voice taut with determination as he snapped his phone shut and shoved it into his pocket.

He must have been speaking to Pierre on the phone, who else could it have been? My eyes followed him as he settled into a chair, his movements deliberate and tense. He began rifling through the paperwork in the office table drawers, a feverish urgency in his search. One drawer was locked, but that didn't stop him; he snatched a knife from the kitchen and forced it open with a sharp, metallic crack. I was never privy to what secrets they both hid in those drawers, but he extracted some folders with a determined air and flicked through them with a fervour that suggested desperation. Suddenly, something snagged his attention; he paused, his breath quickening, and began snapping photos of the documents housed in a manila folder with his phone, as if capturing evidence of some unspeakable truth. When he finished, he shoved the files back into the drawer, his motions hurried and reckless, before getting up and storming out of the house, leaving an unsettling silence in his wake.

I approached the window to confirm his departure and watched as he strolled down the street toward the town centre. Once he was out of sight, I carefully made my way down the stairs. Just as I was about to exit, curiosity got the better of me, and I decided to check what he had been examining in the office.

Mimicking his actions, I sat in the chair, opened the drawer, and took out the same folder, peering inside. It contained a draft report by Harold Kemp titled "DELTA". The first page declared

"PRIVATE AND CONFIDENTIAL"

in large letters, and the next listed various international companies from Boston, London, New York, and even one located in Belgium, along with their addresses and contact information. Unsure of the nature of these businesses, I quickly snapped photos of as many pages as possible with my phone. I returned the folder to the drawer as dusk was falling, and I didn't want to linger there after dark. Besides, I could review the contents later, and I wasn't sure who else might show up at the house. Just as I was about to replace the folder, I noticed a handwritten address on a notepad: 24 Rue Saint Benoit, 6th Arr., Paris 75006. I slipped it into my pocket along with a hundred euros lying on the desk, figuring it might come in handy.

The hotel stood as my only sanctuary, and I made my way back with urgency. My bag offered meagre contents—a half-empty bottle of water—and my stomach growled with a fierce hunger. Desperation drove me to pick up an instant noodle meal, the kind that merely demanded the addition of water. Hardly a feast, but in this moment, choice was a luxury I couldn't afford.

Chapter 14

The last time I saw Camille was just a week ago on Friday morning, standing under the soft glow of our porch light as she chatted about her plans. She mentioned she was taking the kids to visit her sister in the enchanting city of Paris. The anticipation sparked in her eyes as she explained her plan to embark on the journey on Friday evening, right after work. She described the drive as a scenic one, taking less than three hours through the rolling countryside. In contrast, I mused that if I were in Ireland, I'd have to meticulously prepare for such a trip a week in advance. Yet, Camille, with her air of nonchalance and ease, said she was quite accustomed to it. She painted a picture of her sister, a dedicated primary school teacher, who was settled in the heart of Paris with her husband and their lively twins. I found it a bit peculiar that Camille didn't seek my help with the children for the trip, yet a sense of relief washed over me at the thought of having the entire week to myself, a rare opportunity I intended to savour. During this time, Pierre, ever the early riser, wasn't around much; he left before the sun painted the sky with colours and typically didn't return until the stars were twinkling high above, making it the perfect scenario for some solitude and self-indulgence.

On Saturday morning, the start of my kid-free week, I woke up as the first light of dawn softly coloured the sky with shades of pink and orange. As dawn began to break, I made my way to Central Station while the city slowly shook off the remnants of sleep. The streets were serene, bathed in the soft, golden light of early morning. A gentle hush enveloped the area, as the majority of workers, who resided in the suburbs, had already departed after wrapping up their work week on Fridays. The usual hustle and bustle were noticeably absent, leaving behind an unusual calm that lingered in the cool morning air.

There, I boarded a sleek, modern train bound for Bruges, a charming city nestled just over an hour to the north, renowned for its picturesque allure and historic charm. As the train glided effortlessly along the gleaming steel tracks, I felt a growing sense of anticipation bubbling within me, the rhythmic hum of the wheels, a comforting lullaby that soothed my thoughts. The landscapes outside blurred into a tapestry of verdant fields and quaint villages, each scene a fleeting tableau of the countryside. I was being carried closer to Bruges, affectionately known as the "Venice of the North", a moniker that hinted at its enchanting beauty. The city, with its intricate network of canals, seemed to promise a journey back in time. Its serene waterways wove gracefully through the heart of the historic centre, reflecting the centuries-old architecture that lined their banks and offering a glimpse into the rich tapestry of its storied past, where cobblestone streets and medieval buildings whispered tales of yore.

Eager to immerse myself in the city's enchanting atmosphere, I had prudently booked a canal tour online the day before, securing a spot on the nine o'clock excursion. This early preparation spared me the hassle of arranging it on the day. As I arrived, the city greeted me with its serene beauty, quite literally embraced by water that mirrored the medieval architecture lining its banks. The canals, like delicate threads, showcased Bruges' rich heritage, inviting me to explore its timeless charm. The Belfry Tower was another must-see spot on my itinerary, located right in the city centre. This fifteenth-century world heritage site was famous for its stunning bell concerts. You could always tell when the bells were about to ring because crowds would start gathering. According to what I read, the bells chimed at 6am, noon, and again at 6pm, so I made sure not to miss it. I also tackled the three hundred sixty-six steps to the top, and the effort paid off with an incredible view of the rugged cityscape below. Although the city limited the number of people who could climb the tower, leading to long queues, I didn't mind at all.

For a late lunch, I headed to L'Estaminet, a favourite among the locals. This charming and restaurant had a warm, inviting vibe. The downside was that they didn't accept reservations, so I had to wait once more for a seat. The bistro was famous for its oven-baked spaghetti topped with a crispy cheese gratin. The meal was incredible, and I left not a single bite on my plate.

My day trip to Bruges flew by, and soon enough, I found myself on the train heading back to Brussels. Although I was exhausted, I wasn't quite ready to return home when the train arrived at Central Station. I decided to grab a Belgian waffle from one of the numerous street vendors around the city. These waffles are a type of fast food, perfect for eating on the move, made from a deep-fried pancake batter and often topped with apple compote, caramel sauce, whipped cream, and a dash of cinnamon. Personally, I preferred mine simply dusted with powdered sugar. Just as I sat down on a public bench and finished eating it I noticed someone looking at me.

A warm voice called out, "Bonjour, mademoiselle," prompting me to turn. A man stood there, watching me with a relaxed, open expression. His shoulder-length hair framed a face lit by a friendly smile—one that, for reasons I couldn't explain, put me instantly at ease.

"Bonjour, Je m'appelle Luca, et le vôtre? » he asked.

"Laura," I answered.

I was a little surprised and somewhat anxious that a complete stranger was talking to me, but I made an effort to conceal my uneasiness.

"Oh, you're English," he remarked.

"No, I'm Irish," I corrected him.

"Sorry, excuse me," he said with the limited English he had, and then invited me to have a coffee with him.

I hesitated for only a moment before the thought nudged its way in—Go on, Laura. You only live once, so why not? Maybe it was the way the sunlight spilled over the rooftops or the trace of warmth in his smile, but something in me softened.

Before I fully registered for the shift, we were seated at a small wrought-iron table outside one of the cafés that hugged the edge of the Grand Place. The cobblestones beneath our feet still held the day's warmth, and the square around us buzzed with quiet energy, tourists admiring the gilded façades, the clink of glasses from nearby tables, a street musician playing a soft, meandering tune on a violin.

A waiter swept past with effortless charm, leaving behind the scent of espresso and buttery pastries. I leaned back in my chair, letting the noise and colour of the square wash over me. Whatever this moment was—spontaneous or strange, it felt like something I didn't want to interrupt just yet.

Luca shared that he hailed from the sun-drenched city of Naples, nestled in the vibrant south of Italy. For the past five years, however, he had called the bustling heart of Brussels home, where he lived with his brother. His meticulous attention to personal grooming was unmistakable; it seemed he dedicated more time to his reflection than I ever did, his hair expertly styled with gel, each strand perfectly in place, and his shoes gleaming as if polished by a craftsman. With a touch of pride, he revealed that he donned the apron as one of the chefs at a quaint little restaurant situated just on the outskirts of the city, where he infused dishes with the rich flavours of his homeland.

I had seldom encountered anyone who gazed at me with such piercing intensity, and when our eyes locked, I couldn't help but avert my gaze, feeling a strange mixture of intrigue and discomfort. Italian men had a reputation for being flirtatious, a stereotype that was vividly illustrated when the waitress arrived with our steaming coffees. As she gracefully walked away, Bruno's eyes followed her, taking in every detail with a nonchalant sweep that appeared entirely second nature to him, as if he were blissfully unaware of his own actions.

"Would you like to go out for dinner? I know a great restaurant nearby that serves fantastic food," he suggested smoothly, exhaling a curl of smoke from his cigarette that lazily drifted upwards and mingled with the ambient air.

"I would love to, but I have to work, and it doesn't leave me much free time, I'm sorry," I replied, politely declining. I wasn't about to become just another fleeting conquest in his romantic escapades, no matter how alluring he seemed with his charming demeanour and captivating eyes.

"Well, can I at least have your number so I can call you sometime? I promise I don't bite," he insisted, pulling his phone from his pocket with a hopeful gleam in his eyes.

"Why don't I take your number instead, and I'll call you when I'm free?" I replied with a sly smile; fully aware he might expect a brush-off from this charismatic stranger.

"D'accord—okay, you win," he said with a laugh, lifting both hands in mock surrender. The sound burst out of him light and unguarded, like a sudden rush of joy that caught even him by surprise.

I handed him my phone, and he tapped in his number, watching me closely. I made a point of showing him as I saved it, sensing he needed the reassurance—his eyes wide, almost disbelieving, brimming with anticipation.

"Merci for the coffee. I had a lovely time," I said, feeling the warmth of his presence as he leaned in, pressing a kiss to each cheek in a lingering farewell. It was a silent signal that the evening had reached its end, and it was time for me to head home.

Chapter 15

That week slipped away like sand through fingers, disappearing in the blink of an eye. Before I knew it, Friday had arrived, swiftly followed by the gentle dawn of Saturday. Yet, there was still no sign of Camille and the children. Normally, I wasn't one to fret, my mind usually a calm sea, but I had expected her return by now or, at the very least, a phone call to inform me of a trip extension. The house felt unusually quiet, an absence that seemed to echo through each room like a haunting melody. Growing increasingly uneasy, a sense of restlessness creeping into my bones, I decided to reach for my phone. I needed to call her mobile, hoping to hear her familiar voice and ease the gnawing uncertainty that had taken root in my mind.

I dialled her number, pressing the phone to my ear as the ringing tone reverberated in the stillness of the room. Each ring seemed to stretch into eternity, a prolonged chime that heightened my anticipation and anxiety, though no answer came. Finally, the call switched to her voicemail, and I heard the familiar automated message, cold and impersonal, filling the air where her voice should have been.

"Bonjour, vous êtes bien sur la messagerie de Camille. Je ne peux pas répondre pour le moment. Merci de laisser un message après le bip," the recording intoned, Camille's voice calm and collected.

"Hey Camille, it's Laura," I started, my voice betraying a hint of uncertainty. "I hope I'm not interrupting, but I was just wondering when you'll be back. If you could give me a call to let me know, that would be great. Talk to you soon, I guess. Bye," I finished, the emptiness of the voicemail lingering around me, leaving me unsure if I really wanted to hear back or just wanted to sit with the quiet a little longer.

When Sunday morning broke, an overwhelming sense of dread

engulfed my mind, casting a dark pall over my thoughts. Camille's silence was a deafening roar in my ears, amplifying my fears and planting a leaden weight in the depths of my chest. Camille hadn't provided any other contacts, which at first seemed sensible since I only needed her direct details. But now, that glaring lack of information felt like a gaping chasm. Suddenly, a bolt of memory struck—a crumpled scrap of paper buried deep in my pocket. It held an address for an apartment in Paris — possibly her sister's haven. I vaguely recalled Camille mentioning she lived in the vibrant Latin Quarter, or maybe it was the sixth arrondissement. From what I understood, Saint Benoit lay nestled in that vicinity.

Anxiety clawed at me with unyielding ferocity. Were Camille and the children caught in some unforeseen crisis? Why didn't she reach out, asked for help? Maybe she couldn't. Maybe she was trapped, needing me but unable to call.

A fierce determination surged within me, crashing like a storm against the walls of doubt. I had to go. I had to see for myself what waited behind that Parisian door, and whether the truth would meet me there.

Chapter 16

The trains from Brussels were so frequent that I didn't even need to book a ticket in advance. The journey from Brussels Midi to my destination took just under an hour and a half, a smooth and swift passage through the heart of the countryside. As the train sped along, I was greeted by a tapestry of rolling hills that undulated like gentle waves, interspersed with vast expanses of corn and wheat fields swaying in the breeze. Vineyards stretched out endlessly, their neat rows of vines promising the bounty of upcoming harvests. I had become quite adept at navigating the train systems and confidently knew that Gare de l'Est was the nearest train station in Paris to the bustling and charming sixth quarter.

What can I say about Paris? The city exceeded all my expectations and more, surpassing anything I could have imagined. Unlike other urban landscapes, Paris exuded an air of elegance, rich with history, sophistication, and an innate self-assurance that seemed woven into its very fabric. The way women moved through the streets was like witnessing a live fashion show, each step a graceful glide, as if they were models on a runway. The iconic buildings and monuments, with their majestic facades and timeless grandeur, served as a breathtaking backdrop, silently applauding their every movement.

I took a brisk ride on the Mairie D'issy-Metro, commonly referred to as Metro twelve, to reach the bustling Rue Saint Benoit. The train rattled along the tracks, its rhythmic clatter echoing through the dimly lit tunnels. As I emerged onto the lively street, I passed the elegant facades of buildings marked with numbers eighteen, twenty, twenty-two, and finally, twenty-four. My heart sank with confusion. This couldn't be right. I retrieved a crumpled piece of paper from my pocket that clearly stated twenty-four, yet when I lifted my gaze, I was met not with an apartment but with the grand entrance of the Crystal Hotel. Its polished glass doors reflected the vibrant cityscape behind me. Had I squandered my precious time and money only to end up here by mistake? There had to be a compelling reason this address was tucked away in the desk drawer. Resolute, I stepped into the opulent lobby, where the air was scented with a subtle blend of fresh lilies and polished wood. Approaching the reception, I was greeted by a tall, slender man clad in an impeccably tailored three-piece uniform, a gleaming name tag pinned to his lapel reading Phillipe. He was absorbed in his tasks, his fingers dancing over the keys of a computer, seemingly oblivious to my presence. But I was determined not to be overlooked, my curiosity urging me to uncover the mystery behind this elusive address.

"Excusez-moi monsieur, pouvez-vous anglaise?" I enquired with a hopeful tone.

"Yes, miss, I do speak English. How may I assist you?" he replied, looking up from his computer screen with a courteous yet somewhat preoccupied expression.

"I'm wondering if there's a guest here by the name of Camille Dubois," I enquired, attempting to keep my tone relaxed.

"I'm sorry, mademoiselle, I can't divulge that type of information, as our guests value their privacy," he replied, his tone firm yet apologetic.

"Oh, I understand, that's too bad," I replied, pretending to be disappointed. "I'm actually her assistant, and I've lost my phone, so I can't get in touch with her." (Quick thinking was necessary.) "If she's staying here, could I leave a note with you for her? Would that be alright?" I said, rummaging through my bag for a pen, crafting a story that was as fiction as it was pressing.

"Okay, here's some paper and an envelope," he said, offering a small stack of crisp, white sheets and a neatly arranged row of envelopes. His voice was polite but carried a hint of urgency. "If you don't mind, there are guests waiting behind you to check in, so could you take a seat in the lobby while you write?" He gestured towards a seating area adorned with plush armchairs and soft lighting, inviting a sense of comfort and calm. As he spoke, he motioned for the next person in line to step forward, maintaining the smooth flow of guests in the bustling reception area.

I nodded and moved to a plush armchair in the corner of the lobby, the soft hum of conversation and the distant clinking of glassware creating a gentle background symphony. I sat there, staring at the blank page in front of me, my mind as empty as the sheet. I clicked the pen up and down, the sound echoing in my ears, until finally, I scribbled:

Camille, please call me on 0612 345678 when you get this message, it's Laura. I'm in Paris, I need to talk with you.

It wasn't much, but it was the best I could manage.

I nodded with satisfaction as I placed the note paper into the envelope and returned it to the concierge. Just as I was about to pick up my bag from the chair, something startling caught my attention.

A young woman, appearing to be in her twenties, was nonchalantly strolling out the door, with my bag in tow like it was the most natural thing in the world. Her dirty blonde hair, tousled and carefree, framed her face and cascaded down to her shoulders beneath the snug fit of a black beanie. She was clad in dark cargo pants with pockets bulging slightly, and a fitted long-sleeved top that complemented her slender frame. A rugged-looking backpack was slung casually over one shoulder, completing her effortlessly cool ensemble.

"Stop!" I shouted, my voice piercing the air and reverberating through the spacious lobby.

She paused for a split second, casting a sharp glance my way before launching into a full-blown sprint towards the exit, nearly bowling over a middle-aged man who stood waiting patiently in line to check in. Just outside the hotel, she hesitated for the briefest moment, her eyes flicking wildly left and right, before decisively turning right and tearing down the bustling street. My heart thundered in my chest as I bolted after her, my voice hoarse as I shouted for her to stop, but she charged ahead with relentless determination, clearly knowing the path like the back of her hand. She tore onto a lively street swarming with restaurants, weaving through a chaotic maze of tables and chairs, where patrons dined under the blazing afternoon sun. Heads whipped around as she bulldozed her way through, shoving chairs aside with ruthless abandon and crashing into a waiter mid-service, launching dishes into the air and sending food scattering across the pavement like shrapnel.

Patrons in the restaurant gasped in shock as the maître d', clearly unimpressed, yelled in frustration at the disorderly event.

"Regardez où vous vas, espèce de fille stupide," he exclaimed, before turning to apologise profusely to the diners at the table.

Meanwhile, she didn't spare a glance back and sprinted recklessly across the bustling street, her movements a blur against the chaotic backdrop.

She narrowly dodged a speeding taxicab and a massive tour bus, and for a heart-stopping moment, I was certain she would be hit. The traffic came to a jarring halt as the tour bus skidded with a deafening screech, missing her by mere inches. I pursued her with urgency, my heart pounding, as she darted onto a narrow, cobblestone street cloaked in the shadows of towering buildings, casting an ominous and foreboding aura. The street plummeted down a steep flight of at least forty steps toward the famous River Seine. Along the riverbank, the air buzzed with life as stalls overflowed with local artists showcasing everything from vivid replicas of Van Gogh masterpieces to whimsical prints. You could even have your likeness sketched or a playful caricature created. I caught a glimpse of her in the distance, but the throng of tourists was an impenetrable sea, making it maddeningly difficult to track her. She kept glancing back, a flicker of anxiety in her eyes, ensuring I was still on her trail. Breathless, I paused just long enough to catch my breath before plunging back into the dense crowd, determined to reach her. She seemed to believe she'd lost me, her pace slowing to a casual stroll away from the throng, but I saw her heading toward the metro station across the street, and my resolve only intensified as I continued the chase. I boarded Line 1 at Montgomery; the map etched into my memory now from survival rather than sightseeing.

The Paris metro stations stood out unmistakably, adorned with prominent signs that proudly proclaimed "Metropolitan" or "Metro" in bold, large letters. These signs acted as beacons, guiding travellers to their subterranean destinations. However, accessing the underground trains required navigating a descent down a steep, winding staircase, a daunting task for anyone needing assistance. As I followed her down the steps, the cool air of the metro enveloping us, I tried to keep pace. Yet, much to my dismay, amidst the bustling crowd and the echo of hurried footsteps, I lost sight of her. I boarded Line 1 at Montgomery; the map etched into my memory now from survival rather than sightseeing.

"Que veuillez vous?" a voice spoke from behind me.

It was her; she had some sort of knife or object pointing and pushing into my back.

"Ne bouge pas," she commanded.

I was terrified; I'd never been in a situation like this before and had no idea what to do.

"I just want my bag back, that's all," I finally managed to say.

"Oh, so you speak English. You're persistent, aren't you, always chasing after me? So, how much is it worth to you?"

"Please, I don't want any trouble. I need my bag. It has all my stuff in it, and I don't have any other money or a phone with me," I pleaded.

"So, did you find who you were looking for at the hotel? I heard you talking to the man at the desk," she said, pressing the knife into my back again.

"No, I didn't find them. I don't even live here; I came all the way from Brussels to see if I could find her," I replied.

"We're going for a little ride. I wouldn't try anything if I were you," she warned.

She led me down the station to the metro line, and we boarded a train heading north of the city. I had no idea where we were going, but before I knew it, she urged me to get off at Saint-Denis station on the thirteenth line.

"Where are we going?" I asked.

Chapter 17

We walked awkwardly down a few streets, our footsteps echoing softly against the pavement, until we arrived at a towering apartment building that had certainly seen grander days. Its faded facade and chipped paint spoke of years gone by. Groups of men and children clustered around the entrance, their presence unsettling as they scrutinised our every move with keen eyes. They shouted phrases in French, their voices bouncing off the surrounding walls; though I couldn't decipher their words, the tone was unmistakably far from friendly. She, however, appeared completely unfazed, tossing back replies with casual confidence as she rummaged through her backpack to retrieve her keys.

With a gentle creak, the door unlocked, inviting us into a dimly lit lobby that exuded an air of aged elegance. The elevator, bearing a forlorn "out-of-order" sign hanging at an awkward angle, compelled us to climb the four flights of stairs. Each step reverberated with a subtle echo, accompanied by the whisper of fatigue that seemed to cling to the walls. At last, we arrived at her apartment door at the far end of the narrow hallway, marked with the number four hundred and one in slightly tarnished brass. She expertly manoeuvred two separate keys, their metallic teeth catching the light as they slid into the locks, granting us entry. Once inside, she swiftly re-engaged both locks with the ease of routine, securing the door with a solid security bar that settled against the handle with a resolute metallic clink, ensuring our sanctuary.

I watched as she carelessly tossed her keys onto a small, weathered wooden table, their metallic jingle resonating like a faint chime in the tranquil room. She shrugged off her hoodie, revealing a face etched with fatigue, and made her way to the refrigerator. Its door creaked open, casting a cool glow that bathed her features in a soft, pale light. Inside, the shelves were sparsely populated, with a few scattered items that whispered of limited culinary choices, their humble presence a testament to the modest options available for her next meal.

"Well, are you going to return my bag?" I asked again, my voice tinged with impatience, as I stood under the dim overhead light that cast long shadows across the room.

"I think we can make a deal, don't you agree?" she suggested, her eyes glinting with a hint of mischief as she leaned casually against the worn wooden counter.

"What do you mean? Besides my bag, there's nothing you have that I need," I replied, crossing my arms defiantly, though a sliver of curiosity crept into my tone.

"You were looking for a French woman and some children at the hotel, right? I can help you with that," she said, her lips curling into a knowing smile that hinted at secrets untold.

"Camille, you've seen her, when and where?" I asked, my disbelief evident as I stepped closer, a flicker of hope igniting within me.

"Yes, I saw her just a few days ago," she confirmed, her voice smooth and confident. "But she wasn't alone and seemed to be in a rush. For more information, though, it'll cost you," she stated, her gaze steady and unwavering, as if she held all the cards in this unexpected game.

"How do I know you are not lying to me; you could have just overheard me speaking to the hotel manager enquiring about her and made this whole thing up," I replied.

"She had on a long blue coat with a Prada handbag." She smiled.

Only then I realised she was telling me the truth as that is what she was wearing when she left for Paris.

"I even know where she went everyday but that's for me to know at this stage. I can help you, but you have to do something for me in return. She looked up.

"What would that be?" I said as I tried not to appear too nervous.

"I need you to get something for me from an old acquaintance, I'd do it myself, but we didn't part under friendly circumstances and the more I think about it, you would be perfect for it." She smirked.

"What do you need me to get?" I knew she had me over a barrel and she knew it too.

"So, we are in agreement then?" she said as she held her hand up towards me.

"I don't even know your name," I said as my hand met hers.

"Bridgette, and you are Laura, aren't you." It was more of a statement than a question. How did she know that? I wondered.

We sealed the agreement with a handshake, left her apartment, and took the metro to Boliver, located east of the city, a journey of roughly thirty minutes. I boarded Line 1 at Montgomery; the map etched into my memory now from survival rather than sightseeing.

When we exited the station, we pulled up at a restaurant type bar place called Combat which was on the corner.

"So Laura here is the deal. I need you to get friendly with a guy called Benoit in there who works behind the bar. Flirt with him and go back to his place, which isn't far from here, when he's finished his shift in a couple of hours," she explained.

"Wait a second, you don't expect me to sleep with him, do you? Because there is no way I'm doing that," I butted in.

"No, idiot," she said in her thick French accent. "When you get to his apartment, grab my cat and put it in my bag and quickly leave, got it?" she answered.

"A cat. You want me to steal a stupid cat for you?" I shook my head in disbelief.

"It's not a stupid cat, it's mine and I want it back and he won't return it to me. He knows how much I love it and he's doing this to spite me. Anyway, he hates Gabrielle," she warmly said after mentioning her name.

"What if he doesn't ask me to come back with him?" I put it to her.

"You're an attractive girl; you are more of his type than I am. He won't be able to help himself but ask you back, but don't come across too desperate or you'll blow it," she announced.

"Wait, what about you? Where will you be?" I enquired.

"I'll wait outside the building for you when you leave his apartment," she explained.

Chapter 18

The Combat Bar nestled itself at the cusp where two bustling streets converged, its structure gracefully curving to meet the asphalt embrace. I settled into a seat at the far end of the bar, where the ambiance was both lively and tranquil, and my eyes wandered to the clock on the wall, its hands marking the hour as seven o'clock. The bar was alive with a comfortable hum of chatter, filled just enough to create a pleasant buzz without overwhelming the senses. As I scanned the room, my gaze quickly landed on him. He stood out, tall and slender, with short dark hair that framed his face, complemented by a neatly trimmed goatee. He moved with ease and purpose, having just delivered a tray of drinks to a couple nestled at a table in the corner, and now he was making his way back to the bar, weaving through the patrons with practiced grace.

"Bonjour mademoiselle, voulex-vous boire quelque chose?" he enquired with a smile.

I ordered a glass of the cheapest wine I could find being served by him.

"Is someone joining you?" he enquired while filling my glass. I couldn't help but observe the tattoos running down his arms and a handcrafted leather bracelet on his wrist.

"I was, but it seems I've been stood up, so not anymore," I said with a smile.

"His loss, really. I wouldn't have stood you up," he replied with a wink. "I'm Benoit, and you?"

"Laura," I replied as we shock hands.

As the evening progressed, the bar's bustling energy gradually dwindled, the lively chatter softening to an intimate murmur. The dim lighting cast a warm glow, creating an inviting atmosphere. We exchanged words between his rounds of expert mixing and serving drinks to the patrons, his movements fluid and assured. I found myself feeling increasingly at ease, though a part of me was acutely aware of stepping beyond my usual boundaries.

"What are you doing later?" he asked, his voice low and inviting as he leaned over the polished wooden bar. His eyes met mine with a direct and unwavering gaze, a hint of intrigue in his expression.

"I mean, I don't live far from here if you would like to come back to my place for a drink?" His proposal hung in the air, charged with the potential for adventure and the unknown.

"I'm certain you have more important things to do than attempt to act casual as possible, and I'm sure you say that to every girl," I chuckled in response to him.

"No, just you. How about it? I'll make a deal with you: you can leave anytime, no obligations, I swear," he said, drawing an "X" over his heart with his finger.

I agreed, and we left together once he handed over his shift to his female coworker, who would be closing for the night. I couldn't shake the feeling that there was some history between them, perhaps a brief fling that hadn't developed further. He was right about living close by, as it took us just a ten-minute walk from the bar to reach his apartment. When he opened the door, I glanced around, but Bridgette was nowhere to be seen; I just hoped she was keeping an eye on me.

His apartment featured an open-plan layout. A two-seater couch sat invitingly in the centre of the living area with the kitchen overlooking the space, its gleaming countertops and modern appliances visible from every angle. To the left, the bedroom awaited, its neatly made bed and organised shelves exuding an unexpected sense of order. Alongside it lay the bathroom, equally pristine, all of which was surprisingly tidy for a guy's place, a pleasant departure from the usual chaotic bachelor pad.

"What would you like to drink?" he asked, opening the fridge.

"I'm not picky, anything's fine," I answered.

"Relax and make yourself at home. I'll mix you something special; after all, I am a bartender," he chuckled, amused by his own humour.

I settled onto the sofa and admired the stunning nighttime view of the city from the living room.

"Merde, tu m'as presque fait trebucher sur ton stupide chat," he suddenly exclaimed from the kitchen, startling me.

"Sorry, it's that pesky cat; it nearly made me fall," he clarified.

"Oh, so you're a fan of animals," I remarked, anticipating his response.

"Let's just say it's an unwanted gift I'm stuck with," he replied as he approached and sat beside me.

At that moment, an overwhelming tsunami of anxiety slammed into me as he aggressively shoved a drink into my hand. I took a sip, and the fiery burn of vodka, tangled with something cloyingly sweet and a piercing hint of lime, violently assaulted my senses. Without warning, his fingers clawed into my hair, a shocking invasion that electrified every nerve. Instinctively, I recoiled with force, and my drink exploded from my grasp, drenching his jeans in a chaotic, furious splash.

"Merde, qu'est-ce qui se passe?" he shouted.

"I'm really sorry; I have no idea how that happened. I didn't intend to spill it everywhere, but you just startled me," I explained.

"Don't worry about it," he said as he looked down at the damage.

"I have to get out of these clothes anyway. Just give me a second and I'll change and be right back," he said as he got up and entered the bathroom.

He left the door slightly ajar, allowing a sliver of light to spill into the dimly lit hallway. As he began to undress, his movements were deliberate, almost as if choreographed, possibly intending for me to catch a glimpse of his transformation from afar. However, my thoughts were elsewhere, preoccupied with matters that held my attention more firmly than the scene unfolding before me.

"Gabrielle, Gabrielle," I called out.

Where have you gone, you stupid cat? Suddenly, she leaped onto my lap from the side of the couch. I figured she must have hurried over because it had been a while since she last heard her name.

"How do you know my cat's name?" Benoit yelled from the bathroom. "I don't recall ever telling you that."

"Didn't you? You must have," I responded.

Had I just given myself away? Panic surged through me as I pondered the possibility. I swiftly grabbed her, feeling the resistance as she wriggled in my grasp, clearly reluctant to be confined. The bag seemed impossibly small, and for a fleeting moment, I doubted she would fit. But there was no time for hesitation. I manoeuvred her into the bag, zipping it up with urgency. My heart pounded as I made a beeline for the door, my hand trembling slightly as I reached for the handle and began to open it, each movement deliberate and tense.

"Where do you think you're going?" a voice bellowed from behind me, filled with an urgency that sliced through the air like a knife.

I didn't waste a second and bolted out the door, my heart

pounding in my chest. I sprinted towards the lift, frantically jabbing every button, my breath hitching as I silently begged for one to open. But then, he emerged from his doorway, his footsteps thundering after me. Desperation clawed at me, and without a pause, I flung open the door to the staircase, my feet pounding down the steps in a wild, reckless descent. He was hot on my heels, but I pushed myself harder, adrenaline surging, until I burst into the lobby. My panic hit a crescendo when the automatic doors at the entrance stood stubbornly shut. I was frantic, darting back and forth, desperately trying to trigger the sensor, my every movement a plea for escape. My fingers fumbled. I wasn't trained for this, I was improvising with every breath.

I scanned the dimly lit corridor with urgency, my heart racing as I spotted him emerging like a shadow from the staircase exit. From the corner of my eye, I caught sight of the button that could be my salvation, positioned tantalizingly close to the exit. Driven by a surge of desperation, I dashed toward it and slammed my palm against the button with all my might. The doors groaned open with a mechanical hum, but before I could leap to freedom, his iron grip clamped around my arm, dragging me back into the suffocating darkness of the stairwell. My heart thundered in my chest when, suddenly, a blur of motion erupted behind him. Someone lunged forward and struck him with brutal force at the back of his head. I spun around, adrenaline coursing through my veins, to see Bridgette standing over him, wielding a heavy metal object like a weapon. His body collapsed to the ground, a pitiful moan escaping his lips as his fingers came away slick with blood from his wounded head. Bridgette spat something sharp and commanding in French, her words slicing the air with intensity, before delivering a vicious kick to his side.

"Come on, let's move!" she exclaimed, pulling me along as we dashed down the street.

Chapter 19

After that eventful night, we went back to Bridgette's apartment. With nowhere else to go, I accepted her offer to stay there as a thank you for what I had done.

She mentioned that it was pointless to take me to where she'd seen Camille at such a late hour, and that we would head there in the morning.

"Are you hungry? I picked up some food while I was waiting for you," she said.

Bridgette had picked up some cheese, bread, and meat, along with a bottle of wine, and invited me to indulge. Famished, I eagerly accepted the offer. She mentioned I could crash on the couch, which was already set up with a blanket, and then retreated to her room with her cat. I was struck by how different she seemed compared to earlier that evening. Sleep eluded me that night, not just because the couch was uncomfortable, but also because my mind was racing with everything that had happened and how much had changed in the last two days.

"Morning, Laura. Did you sleep well?" Bridgette asked carrying Gabrielle in her arms.

"Yes, thanks," I answered, raising my head from the pillow.

"We should head out soon. I have a busy day ahead, so I'll take you to the places your friend has been visiting," she mentioned.

We embarked on another metro journey back to the vicinity of our hotel, but this time, she drew my attention to an imposing financial building nestled a few streets away. We chose a seat at a quaint café directly facing this architectural marvel. The building was a sleek structure, its facade entirely sheathed in gleaming glass, and it soared gracefully into the sky, likely reaching ten storeys high. The sunlight danced across its surface, creating a dazzling display of reflections and light. I boarded Line 1 at Montgomery; the map etched into my memory now from survival rather than sightseeing.

"So, what's the plan now? Are we just supposed to sit and wait? You could have taken her stuff back at the hotel. Why did you have to trail her all the way here?" I enquired, watching intently.

"Regarde." Before she could respond, she gestured towards the car arriving in front of the building.

Camille gracefully stepped out of the sleek BMW, the door clicking shut behind her. She turned back momentarily and then the car then swiftly accelerated, its engine purring as it disappeared down the street. My mind raced with questions. That wasn't Pierre in the car; who was it? Had I just witnessed something I wasn't meant to see? Was Camille involved in an affair?

"Camille!" I called out.

She spun around, surprised to see me waving at her. I stood up and told Bridgette I'd be back soon.

"I've been searching all over for you. I really need to speak with you," I said.

"Laura, why are you in Paris? How did you find out I was here? I can't talk right now. I'm heading back to Brussels tonight. Can we meet later today? I'll explain everything then, but I'm running late," she replied.

"I thought you were visiting your sister here. Who was that man, and where are the children?" I asked, my gaze fixed intently on her face.

She tried to reassure me with a gentle smile, though I could sense an underlying tension in her eyes. We decided to meet later that evening at her hotel, where she promised to explain everything. As she hurried into the towering glass and steel structure, she cast a quick glance back at me, her expression fleetingly vulnerable. With a swift motion, she pulled out her mobile phone and dialled a number, her fingers deftly tapping the screen. She scanned her pass at the security checkpoint and disappeared into the elevator, leaving me with a swirl of unanswered questions.

"Well, how did that go? I told you I knew where she was," Bridgette said with a big grin on her face.

"Yeah, you sure did," I answered.

Something felt off, yet I couldn't quite put my finger on it. I was torn between wanting to dig deeper immediately and knowing I had to hold off until later to uncover the full truth.

"I appreciate your help, Bridgette. I'm happy you were reunited with your cat, even if the method was rather unorthodox," I said with a smirk.

We exchanged our farewells at the bustling café, the aroma of freshly brewed coffee mingling with the chatter of patrons around us. She handed me back my bag, the fabric worn smoothly from years of use, and leaned in to give me a warm kiss on each cheek. Her lips were soft, and her perfume left a delicate trace in the air, a sweet reminder of our time together.

Since I couldn't meet up with Camille until later in the afternoon, I decided to sit down by the river and soak in the views. After all, it's not every day you find yourself in such a magnificent city, and I haven't had the chance to explore much over the past twenty-four hours. The riverbanks were lined with benches, their wood weathered and warm in the late afternoon sun. I settled onto one and opened my bag to check its contents. Everything was in place: the little money I had left, my phone, a slightly dented water bottle, my jingling keys, and a well-worn notepad with a pen nestled beside it. A grin spread across my face as I flipped through the notepad and found Bridgette's name and mobile number scrawled in with a cheerful smiley face beside it. I sensed that she might be a bit of a loner, lacking a circle of friends, which tugged at my heart. Yet, I hoped that, in some small way, I could be one of those friends for her.

She even took the liberty of charging my phone for me, perhaps out of curiosity or simply to be helpful. I discovered six voicemails: three from Aoife, who sounded extremely worried about my whereabouts, two from unidentified numbers that hung up after reaching voicemail, and the last from Alex, just checking in on me. If only he knew the full story! I arrived at the hotel at four o'clock, as I had arranged with Camille. This time, a woman was at the reception desk, so I sat in the lobby, waiting for Camille to come down from her room. After thirty minutes with no sign of her, I asked the receptionist to inform Camille that I was waiting, but the woman gave me an odd look.

Upon returning to the hotel the female concierge informed me that Madam Dubois checked out mid-afternoon around three o'clock.

"You must be Laura?" she asked.

"Yes, that's right," I responded.

"J'ai laissé un message pour vous," she said, handing me a note before answering the ringing phone.

The note read:

I am sorry Laura; I had to leave. They know you are in here; you are in danger and need to get out of Paris tonight and go back to Brussels quickly!

Her note also explained that I needed to contact an acquaintance of hers who could save me from this mess.

I retreated into the dimly lit public bathroom, the stark reality of my predicament crashing down on me like a tidal wave. As I stepped out into the corridor, a chill ran down my spine, and I froze, my heart hammering wildly in my chest. The voice that reached my ears was unmistakable—it was the same man who had been talking to Pierre on that fateful night. He was now interrogating the receptionist, his voice sharp and demanding, about Camille's whereabouts. I slunk back into the shadows, pressing myself against the cool, textured wall, straining to catch every word. The receptionist, maintaining a calm facade, informed him that I had been there earlier but had since checked out.

His gaze, piercing and calculated, swept across the room with deliberate, predatory intensity, like a hawk searching for its elusive prey. The atmosphere was tense, charged with an undercurrent of threat, as he finally stormed out of the hotel, his footsteps echoing ominously in the quiet lobby. Only when I was absolutely certain he had vanished into the night did I dare to emerge from my hiding place. The receptionist caught my eye, offering a subtle, knowing wink that signaled it was safe. I nodded in return, my silent gratitude palpable in the air between us.

A sense of urgency thrummed through my veins, a relentless pulse driving me forward. I needed to escape to Brussels immediately, the weight of the situation pressing heavily on my shoulders as I moved with purpose toward my destination.

Chapter 20

As the train pulled into the station, I couldn't help but wonder why I didn't just go home, back to Ireland, back to my normal life. I could borrow the money and get on the first flight out of here. I could see my friends and family again, but I could not put them in danger like that. These people could easily find my parents' address and I did not want any harm to come to them, so I had to find a way to end this and get my life back.

I glanced at Camille's note once more, seeing the name **Victor Novak**. Trusting her or this Victor seemed risky, but I had no other option. Camille had also provided his phone number, so I dialled it, my heart racing with the urgency of her plea. The phone rang a few times before he picked up.

"Qui," the voice on the other end of the line said.

His calm and measured voice eased my nerves. Speaking in short, precise sentences, I conveyed the necessity for his immediate assistance. I stumbled for a bit before I replied.

"Hello, I hope it's okay that I'm reaching out. Camille Dubois provided me with your number and mentioned that you could assist me," I said.

There was a pause on the end of the line before he replied.

"Yes, I know who you are, I was expecting your call. We will keep this brief just in case they are listening in. Come to my house, I presume she wrote down the address?" he asked.

"Yes, I have it."

"Good." Then the phone went dead.

Watermael-Boitsfort lay nestled in the southeast quadrant of the city, a haven for the affluent, as evidenced by the grand, stately homes that lined its serene streets. This distinguished suburb brushed against the sprawling expanse of the Sonian Forest, a verdant sanctuary spanning over five thousand hectares. The forest, with its towering trees and whispering leaves, was a must-see on my ever-growing list of places to explore when time allowed. However, with so many captivating destinations vying for my attention, my visit to this lush woodland would have to be postponed for a future day.

Victor's home was situated opposite one of the two rivers in the area. Although not modern, it stood proudly alongside the larger, upscale houses nearby. It was a modest two-storey rendered dwelling with a slated roof and a chimney at its centre. Lacking a doorbell, I knocked on the door and waited, spotting someone through the glass approaching to open it.

"Come on in, Laura!" Victor greeted. He was a man in his mid-fifties, dressed in worn-out jeans and a thick sweater. His face showed a couple of days' worth of stubble, his hair was thin and wispy, and he wore glasses.

"Thanks," I said as I walked past him into the main living space. It wasn't exactly tidy, so he hurriedly cleared some papers and clothes from a chair to make room for me to sit.

"Were you followed?" he demanded sharply, his eyes scanning the street through the window with a laser-like focus.

"No. I mean, I don't think so," I stammered, my voice tinged with uncertainty.

"That's not good enough!" he snapped, turning to me with an intense glare. "You have to be more vigilant, always. You must make absolutely certain that no one is on your tail," he commanded, his words carrying the weight of urgency and a hint of desperation.

"Camille mentioned you could assist me. Can you?" I demanded, my voice edged with desperation.

He leaned forward, eyes penetrating. "We need to start from scratch. Tell me everything. Why are they after you?" His gaze was unwavering as he settled into his seat.

"I don't know," I blurted, panic rising in my chest. "It all happened so fast." Taking a deep breath, I began to unravel the chaotic story. My fingers fumbled. I wasn't trained for this, I was improvising with every breath.

I began working for my host not that long ago and quickly settled into a routine with the kids. Every morning, Camille would take Max to daycare, and I'd pick him up shortly after lunch, around two o'clock. Since Chloe was only six months old, she attended daycare only on Tuesdays and Thursdays, so on those days, I'd pick up both children. I took my French lessons at the Alliance Francaise while they were at daycare, leaving the rest of the time for just Chloe and me. We'd visit the park, or I'd handle some errands for Camille. Everything was running smoothly until three weeks ago, while on the bus after collecting the kids from daycare, I spotted Pierre with Harold Kemp near the European Commission. The children were too engrossed in their toys to notice. When my bus halted at the traffic lights, Pierre saw me, paused mid-conversation, and gave me an unsettling look. I didn't dwell on it and continued with my day.

"That evening, after bathing the kids, I carefully carried little Chloe down the grand staircase, her sleepy eyes half-closed, while Max, her energetic brother, followed closely behind, his footsteps echoing softly against the polished wood. It was time to serve them dinner before they drifted off to sleep. As I reached the foot of the stairs, the gentle murmur of voices floated from the kitchen. I heard Camille's voice, warm and melodic, enquiring about Pierre's business trip. Curiously, he mentioned Dusseldorf, but I saw him in Brussels that day, a detail that puzzled me. I cast a discreet glance towards them. Camille, with her hair tied back, was deftly preparing the evening meal, her hands moving with practiced ease as she recounted the events of her day.

Pierre then approached me, took Chloe from my arms, and asked if any mail had arrived that day. When I told him we hadn't received any, he raised his eyebrows in mild disbelief before breaking into a smile, but it was laced with an unsettling edge, a sinister tension lurking beneath his seemingly pleasant demeanour. As merely the hired help, I tried to brush it off as paranoia, yet unease gnawed at me while I forced myself to return to the children.

His smile was polished, but it didn't reach his eyes. 'You ask a lot of questions, Laura,' he said. 'Curiosity can be dangerous.'

"Continuez s'il vous plait Laura," Victor responded with enthusiasm.

"A couple of days later, on a wet Friday afternoon, just as I was preparing to head out with Chloe to pick up Max, the doorbell rang, cutting through the continuous rain. When I opened the door, there stood a soaked postman, his uniform clinging to him from the downpour. He was about to drop an envelope into the mailbox when our eyes met, and he handed it directly to me instead. Both the envelope and the postman were soaked from the relentless rain. I quickly tucked the envelope into my bag while carefully placing Chloe in the pram. Each tick of the clock reminded me I was running late; Camille would not have been pleased if I missed the bus or risked Chloe getting a chill.

Thankfully, the bus stop was just a few steps from the house, and I managed to arrive in the nick of time. The journey to daycare took a brisk twenty minutes; while Chloe was snugly cocooned under a rain cover in the pram, I grappled with the challenge of holding an umbrella and pushing the pram at once. The rain proved relentless, and despite my best efforts, I ended up dampened by each gust of wind. Desperate for a reprieve, I rifled through my bag searching for something to dry myself with, but all I found was a small face towel that promised little comfort.

I then retrieved the envelope meant for Pierre and, with careful urgency, tried to dry it as best I could.

As I inspected the envelope, I noticed it was strangely bare; no sender's details were visible, and the incessant rain had slackened its seal ever so slightly. Tentatively, I began pulling back the damp, sticky flap when an unexpected surge of guilt halted my progress. Shaking off the fleeting emotion, I resumed opening it and discovered inside a USB flash drive paired with a bank card. What immediately set my mind alight was that the bank card was issued in the name Harold Kemp. My thoughts raced—why would Pierre have something bearing that name? But time was not on my side; with my bus stop fast approaching, I quickly rang the bell to signal the bus driver into action.

Upon reaching the daycare, I spotted Max's familiar figure. Occasionally, his eyes would brighten when he saw me, but today he seemed hesitant to part with his chatty friends and the activities he was absorbed in. And after much gentle coaxing, he finally bid farewell and we headed off into the misty rain, leaving a silence that hung heavily until we reached home.

That evening, once the children were asleep, I retreated to my modest room. I stripped away the day's troubles in a warm, soothing shower, the water cascading over me like a gentle rain of its own. After washing my hair and drying off, I sank into the worn embrace of a two-seater couch whose fabric told the story of many yesterdays. Still, the mysterious flash drive and bank card beckoned my curiosity. I retrieved my laptop, inserted the USB, and watched as the screen flickered to life with half a dozen folders.

"Nothing immediately captured my attention until I clicked on the folder labelled 'photos'. There, a series of images unfolded on the screen, each portraying a single, enigmatic figure. At first, his identity eluded me, but as I scrolled through the snapshots, realisation dawned—it was Harold Kemp. Some photos showed him in solitude, caught in moments of pensive isolation; others depicted him interacting with people in various settings. The most disquieting images, however, were of him inside his own home, engrossed in conversations on his phone or absorbed before his computer screen.

Intrigued yet unsettled, I then navigated to a folder named 'private'. Inside, I found a memo addressed to Mr. Kemp, meticulously written by someone named Son Ngui, a senior software engineer at a major tech company. The note deepened the mystery, leaving me with an unsettling blend of questions and curiosity that would echo in my thoughts long into the night.

PRIVATE & CONFIDENTIAL

Date: 25 April 2021
To: Harold Kemp, Head of Security, Delta Inc.
From: Son Ngui, Senior Software Engineer
I am writing to inform you that I have come across a piece of malicious code which I believe has been planted into our software designed to steal financial information from one of our clients, Transpacific Corp.
I have removed this code however I came across the same code again in the database of a completely different company.
I will provide you with further information once I have reviewed all our clients' databases which will be within a week.
Thank you.

A file from Son, dated a week prior, provided Mr. Kemp with information about at least thirty businesses affected by the same malicious code.

"Did you discover who was behind the code infection in these companies?" Victor asked, passing me a glass of water, aware of my anxiety.

"No, there wasn't any additional information on the USB that I noticed," I replied.

"Where is the USB now, Laura?" he enquired.

"In my bag; when I saw what was on it, I didn't know what to do. If I gave Pierre the package, he would have known that I looked inside of it because the seal was broken, so I pretended I didn't have it at all; but I realised he did know when I heard him talking to that man at the doorway. So that's where it all started and then Harold Kemp was found dead just recently," I stated.

I recounted the entire story, convinced that the same man has been trailing me since then.

Victor remained silent for a moment, clearly pondering his next words.

"Listen, let me investigate Pierre a bit more. I have some friends I can discreetly ask for information," he offered.

"Should I go to the police and report what I know?" I asked.

"No, don't do that. You would be putting yourself in serious danger without sufficient evidence," he warned.

"But I have photos and other things. Are you saying they won't believe me?" I was taken aback.

"People like this don't quit easily, so we need to wait until we have something more substantial," he explained.

Following his suggestion, I departed and made my way back to the hotel, a modest establishment nestled on a quiet side street. I had secured a room there for a few nights, paying in cash to maintain a sense of privacy and ease. The hotel's exterior was unassuming, with its vintage brick facade and a small, welcoming sign that swayed gently in the breeze. Inside, the lobby was warm and inviting, adorned with plush armchairs and softly lit lamps that exuded a comforting glow.

Chapter 21

I know that Victor didn't want me to contact anyone, but I couldn't just wait around for them to find me, so I went online to search for Son Ngui. Where to start? Social media was probably the best, and I had to narrow down my search to the Brussels location as I knew he worked in the city.

Three possible matches came up and I sent them all the same DM.

Hello, I'm fully aware of Harold Kemp and the security breaches at Delta Inc. This matter is urgent, and your assistance is crucial. I implore you to reach out to me immediately. We need to meet as soon as possible.

After sending the message, I found myself obsessively checking for any replies, but none of the recipients had read it yet leaving me in a state of anxious anticipation. To distract myself, I indulged in a much-needed shower, the hot water cascading over me felt like a cleansing waterfall after what seemed like an eternity in the same worn clothes. Fortunately, hotels are always generous with their supply of crisp, fluffy towels. As I lathered my hair with fragrant shampoo, the soothing sensation washed away my tension, and I emerged feeling instantly revitalised and more at ease.

As I strolled back into the bedroom, running a brush through my damp hair, I heard a familiar buzz from my phone resting on the table. It was a message from one of the guys, stating tersely that I had the wrong person. So, that lead had fizzled out. The message to the other Son had been opened, the read receipt glaring back at me, yet there was no reply—perhaps I had targeted the wrong individual once more. I glanced at the clock; its hands pointed to 10:15, and an overwhelming drowsiness weighed heavily on my eyelids. Within mere moments of my head meeting the cool embrace of the pillow, I drifted into a deep and immediate slumber.

When I woke up, I noticed a section of the curtain had come loose from the rail, permitting a stream of soft, golden light to filter into the room. The clock displayed at ten o'clock, and I was taken aback to discover that I had slept a solid eleven hours without interruption. My phone sat on the bedside table, its top light blinking a gentle green, signaling the arrival of a new message. To my amazement, it was from Son, he had finally replied to me!

Meet me at the Atomium Sculpture at midday.

Come alone and don't be late.

The message arrived at two in the morning, and I checked his Facebook page, only to find he hadn't posted anything in over three weeks. The Atomium was located in the northern part of the city, in an area called Laken. It was just a metro ride away; I knew this because it had been on my Brussels to-do list, and I had already checked it off. Exiting Heizel metro on line six, it was just a brief five-minute walk to the Atomium. I arrived early, so I purchased a croissant from a local vendor, took a seat, and watched the world go by. It was a well-visited tourist spot, with people moving between the sculpture and the Mini-Europe attraction.

I glanced at my phone and saw it was already one o'clock. I had been waiting for over an hour with no sign of Son arriving. I decided I would wait just another thirty minutes; if he didn't show, it would be pointless to stay any longer—he must have changed his mind. Just then, my phone pinged.

"Follow me into Mini-Europe beside the Cathedral of Santiago de Compostela in Spai.", it read.

Mini-Europe was a sprawling park brimming with miniature scale models of iconic landmarks from cities scattered across the

European Union. From the Leaning Tower of Pisa, slightly tilted yet perfectly stable, to the majestic ruins of Greece's Acropolis, each model was crafted with intricate detail. In my opinion, it was the kind of place that left a lasting impression after just one visit. After purchasing my ticket and stepping through the gates, I made my way straight to the monuments. The air was filled with the soft murmur of other visitors, and initially, I couldn't spot him among the crowd. But then, a familiar voice echoed from behind me, breaking through the ambient noise.

"Who are you?" a voice asked. Just as I was about to turn around, he added, "Don't look back, just pretend you're a tourist and keep moving." It was clearly him speaking to me.

"I'm the nanny for Pierre Dubois's children in Brussels. It was purely by chance that I stumbled upon the information regarding Harold Kemp and the data breach," I explained, my voice tinged with urgency.

"And how can I be sure you're not working for them? This might be a setup," he replied, his eyes narrowing with suspicion.

"I'm being honest with you; you have to trust me. I didn't choose this," I pleaded, my voice trembling as I wiped the tears that had begun to spill from my eyes, leaving streaks on my cheeks.

There was a tense pause, the air between us heavy with uncertainty, before he stepped forward. His eyes locked onto mine with an intensity that demanded truth.

"Are you certain no one followed you?" he asked, his voice low and serious, as if the weight of the world depended on my answer.

He appeared quite disheveled, his appearance bordering on neglected. He wore a faded denim jacket, it's once vibrant blue now dulled by time, along with a pair of jeans that bore the marks of countless wears and washes. His worn-out white t-shirt, frayed at the collar and stained with faint traces of past spills, clung to him loosely. His hair, slick with oil, lay plastered against his scalp, giving it a greasy sheen that caught the light awkwardly. Beneath his eyes were prominent dark circles, like bruises from sleepless nights, casting shadows that accentuated the weary pallor of his face.

Chapter 22

The office was perched high on the twenty-fifth floor of a sleek, modern skyscraper nestled in the bustling heart of Brussels. Floor-to-ceiling windows framed a breathtaking panorama of the cityscape, letting in shafts of golden sunlight that bathed the room in a warm, radiant glow. The interior boasted a contemporary elegance, with minimalist décor and clean lines that spoke of both precision and style. Amid it all, a polished mahogany desk stood as a centrepiece, its glossy surface reflecting the subtle interplay of light and shadow from the overhead fixtures.

At the head of this commanding space, Marceau, a man as cold and unyielding as stone stepped forward. His tall, sharply tailored suit clung to his athletic frame, every deliberate and measured movement exuding quiet authority. With an unwavering, severe gaze, he fixed his eyes on Pierre as he spoke in a low, cutting tone that resonated with unspoken fury:

"Pierre, your negligence threatens us all," he intoned, punctuating his words with a slow nod and a clenched jaw that brooked no argument. The gravity of his displeasure was palpable, hanging in the air like a dense fog, especially given the precarious situation involving Laura and the sensitive documents at risk.

His frustration boiled over as he demanded, "How is she still slipping through our fingers?" That question erupted from him as suddenly as a storm, the sound of his hand slamming against the polished mahogany desk reverberating off the walls of the dimly lit room. The space was charged with tension, each second heavy with the impending promise of dire consequences. A brief, electric silence followed before he fixed his steely gaze back on Pierre, who now looked visibly uncomfortable, his face betraying the strain of the situation.

Without so much as breaking eye contact, Marceau reached for a half-full bottle of amber liquid and then sat behind his huge desk. The glass clinked softly as he poured himself another drink, the rich aroma of the alcohol mingling with the lingering scent of leather and tobacco smoke that inflected the study, crafting an atmosphere thick with intrigue and impending judgement.

"I guarantee we'll locate her; it's only a matter of time before she makes a mistake and reappears on our radar. We believe she'll…" he began, his tone underscored by an unyielding certainty.

Interrupting his own train of thought with a sharp snap of his voice, he declared, "I won't tolerate excuses or overthinking. She must be found immediately. Is that understood? We have too much to lose if this gets out." His words cut through the air with the precision of a finely honed blade, leaving no room for dissent or hesitation. The urgency in his tone crackled with intensity, an electrifying command that permitted no defiance, charging the atmosphere with a palpable tension.

Marceau continued, his orders growing more precise. "I need surveillance on every single person she's come into contact with since her arrival. Make them talk, squeeze out every drop of information they have. When you come back through that door, she better be with you. Now, GET OUT!" He barked out a sharp, impatient reply, his voice rising with frustration.

Without waiting for a response, he ended the conversation abruptly, snapping the phone back to his ear as another call came through. The screen lit up with a familiar number, one that meant business. His posture straightened, jaw tightening, as he listened intently. Whoever was on the other end had authority, and their words poured in like marching orders, urgent and uncompromising.

With that, all dialogue ceased. Pierre rose from his seat, leaving the confines of the office behind. Outside, a sleek car waited at the building's front entrance, its polished exterior glinting under the city lights, and Pierre climbed into the back seat, the leather interior echoing with the earlier tension.

As the car hummed softly away from the towering edifice, the stranger seated beside Pierre broke the silence with a gentle enquiry. The vehicle glided smoothly over the asphalt, its engine a low, steady purr in the background.

"So, what exactly would you like me to do about this now?" Their voices held a subtle hint of curiosity, each word carefully measured, eyes sharp and inquisitive as they searched Pierre's face for answers. The stranger's gaze was like a pair of finely tuned instruments, probing with an intensity that sought to uncover hidden truths.

A faint smile played on Pierre's lips, a knowing expression that hinted at the plans forming in his mind. He responded, "Let's just say we're planning to visit her friends and discover what information they might have for us." His tone was light, yet beneath it lay a seriousness that hinted at the gravity of their task. His smile was polished, but it didn't reach his eyes. 'You ask a lot of questions, Laura,' he said. 'Curiosity can be dangerous.'

Immediately, the passenger produced a sleek laptop from a padded case, a repository brimming with information and photographs of everyone Laura had encountered since her arrival in Brussels. The device was a treasure trove of data, its screen flickering to life with images and documents that painted a complex web of connections.

"Then you'll need this," the passenger said, handing the device over with a sense of urgency. They gestured toward an image of a girl with long, dark hair, her striking and enigmatic features, identified as Nina. She seemed to hold secrets of her own, locked behind her mysterious gaze. "Let's begin with this one and see what she can reveal to us."

The journey continued, the weight of every detail melding into the mission that lay ahead. The cityscape loomed in the distance, its secrets hidden just beyond the shadows, waiting to be uncovered as the car pressed onward into the unknown.

Chapter 23

I met Nina, another au pair, at one of the Irish clubs. Her English wasn't very good, and I didn't know any German, yet we hit it off surprisingly well. She worked in central Brussels for a single woman with a four-year-old daughter. While my job lasted a full year, her placement was only for six months. The first time we met up outside the club, I went to her house so we could grab coffee at a nearby café. Her living arrangement was quite nice, featuring a double bed, a twin sofa, and a TV mounted on the wall. She even had an en-suite bathroom, which I found myself envying. Since her room was on the ground floor, adjacent to the garage, she could come and go as she pleased without bothering anyone. We started meeting up more often after that, usually for walks, cheap coffee, or just to escape the chaos of our host families. It didn't take long before I felt comfortable enough to drop by unannounced, slipping through the side gate of her host's townhouse like I belonged there.

On this particular day, she was coaxing Loly to eat her lunch.

"You have to finish all your food before you can have any chocolate, Loly," Nina instructed gently, her voice a blend of firmness and warmth.

The dining room was filled with the comforting aroma of homecooked food, and the soft clinking of cutlery against plates provided a soothing background melody. Nina leaned forward slightly, her eyes twinkling with a mix of encouragement and a hint of mischief.

"You have to finish all your food before you can have any chocolate, Loly. Otherwise, I'll be the one in hot water with your mum, more than you might think," Nina explained, encouraging her to eat the rest of her meal.

Nina and Loly were seated at the kitchen table when the doorbell rang. "I wonder who that might be? Finish your food, I'll be back shortly," Nina said as she got up to answer the door.

When she opened the front door, she was greeted by two men in suits standing directly in front of the entrance, obstructing her view of the street. It caught her off guard, as such a sight was unusual in her peaceful cul-de-sac.

"Bonjour, est-ce que je parle à Nina?"

"Qui, that is me, how can I help you?" she nervously responded.

"My name is Inspector Janssen," he introduced himself with a firm but courteous tone, "and my colleague here is Inspector Jacob."

Both men wore the crisp, dark suits typical of federal officers, their badges glinting under the overhead light. "We represent the federal police, specifically the missing persons unit," Janssen continued, his eyes steady and probing. The air in the room seemed to tighten as he reached into his coat, producing his identification with a swift, practised motion. The badge shone briefly as he held it out for Nina to see before tucking it away again.

"Ms. Nina are you familiar with a Mademoiselle Laura Farrell?" he enquired, his voice laced with professional urgency and a hint of compassion.

"Laura? What's happened? Is she ok? What's going on? Is something the matter?" Nina interjected.

"Mademoiselle Farrell has been reported missing by her employers several days ago," the officer stated, his voice carrying a weight of concern as he glanced down at his notepad.

"We're reaching out to her friends to gather any information that might help us locate her. Have you had any recent contact with her or perhaps received any text messages from her?" he enquired, his tone both professional and sincere, as his eyes searched for any hint of recognition or recollection.

"Oh my god, I haven't seen Laura for over a week! It's so unlike her not to text or call me—I was really starting to worry. But then again, I was caught up in a whirlwind trip to Germany with my family for work and only got back late last night. I haven't even had the chance to reach out to her yet!" Nina exclaimed; her voice tinged with urgency.

Loly sprinted to the front door with the urgency of a whirlwind. "I finished every bite of my food; can I have some chocolate now?" she demanded, her voice a mixture of desperation and anticipation as she tugged insistently on the pocket of Nina's trousers.

"Listen, I'm sorry but I have to go back to work now," Nina said as she gently lifted Loly into her arms.

"Thank you, Mademoiselle. If you hear from her, please inform us. Here's my card, and you can reach me at any time. Also, if anything comes to mind that might assist, no matter how minor, don't hesitate to contact me." With that, Inspector Janssen handed Nina a business card.

"Au-revoir, Nina and Loly," he called out as they both walked away. Nina used her leg to close the front door and then rested against it.

"Loly, how did they know your name? I never told them," she murmured, confusion lacing her words. Her mind spun with uncertainty, a knot of unease twisting tighter in her stomach as she recalled that they also knew her address. Laura had no reason to share such personal details with her employers. Her thoughts were like leaves caught in a gust, swirling chaotically as she turned toward the kitchen. The evening light seeped in through the window, casting elongated shadows that seemed to stretch on forever across the tiled floor. With a mix of hesitation and urgency, she reached for her phone, her fingers wavering as she pressed the speed dial for Laura's number, unsure yet needing answers.

"Damn it, it's going to voice message!" Nina exclaimed; her voice tinged with urgency. "Laura, please call me the moment you hear this. It's crucial!" With a heavy sigh, she slammed the phone down, her heart pounding with frustration.

She found her laptop in the living room, opened it, and logged into her Facebook account. She navigated to her Facebook friends and searched for Laura.

"There you are," she murmured, her eyes locking onto the screen as she clicked on Laura's details. The soft glow from the monitor illuminated her face, casting a gentle light across her focused expression. As the page loaded, a wealth of information unfurled before her, each line and image painting a vivid picture of Laura's life.

Laura's most recent post was from more than a week ago, showing her and Chloe feeding ducks at the local pond. Since then, she hadn't posted anything. Nina tried reaching out to Laura through a private message but couldn't determine her last activity. Consequently, she messaged Aoife, whom she knew through Laura, although they weren't particularly close.

"Hello Aoife, it's Nina, Laura's friend from the club. Some people came to my house claiming to be police officers, asking if I knew Laura's whereabouts. It seems she hasn't been seen for more than a week. Have you seen her recently?" Nina pressed the send button.

As Nina sprang up from the couch, her heart raced when she spotted the same men lurking in an unmarked car. Her pulse quickened as she lifted the blind and caught one of them furiously snapping pictures of the house. The air crackled with tension, and the moment Nina's eyes locked onto theirs; they sped away in a flurry, tyres screeching against the pavement, leaving a cloud of dust in their wake.

Chapter 24

Aoife leisurely strolled along the lively and bustling streets of Brussels, weaving her way through the vibrant tapestry of city life toward a quaint little café named Au Soleil. Nestled snugly in the heart of the city, this charming establishment was situated on the picturesque Rue du Marche au Charbon. The café's exterior was a delightful sight, adorned with vibrant flower boxes overflowing with a riot of colourful blooms, their petals dancing in the gentle caress of the wind. An inviting wooden sign, carved with intricate details, swung softly in the breeze, beckoning passersby with its rustic charm and promise of warmth and comfort within.

Nina shouted, "Aoife, over here!" Her voice cutting through the soft murmur of conversation in the snug café. She waved eagerly from a small round table tucked into the back corner, where the light from a nearby lamp bathed the area in a glow. As Aoife drew near, the scent of freshly brewed coffee and baked pastries surrounded her. They greeted each other with kisses on each cheek, a customary gesture that felt as natural to them as the embrace of an old companion.

"Thanks for meeting me here, Aoife. I thought it would be better that we talk in person and not over the phone," Nina explained as she took a seat.

"That's no issue at all, I totally agree. I just got myself a coffee. Would you like one too?" Nina signaled for the waiter.

"Un café s'il vous plaît," Aoife requested in French, her voice a harmonious blend of gentleness and assurance as she addressed the waiter. Her eyes took in the quaint charm of the café, where the air was rich with the inviting aroma of freshly brewed coffee mingling with the delicate, buttery scent of pastries. The soft murmur of conversations floated around her, a gentle hum that blended with the rhythmic clattering of porcelain cups, creating a warm, comforting symphony. As she waited for her steaming cup of solace, the café's ambiance wrapped around her like a familiar embrace.

Aoife got straight to the point as soon as Nina sat down. "I'm really worried about Laura," she admitted, her voice tinged with urgency. "The last time I saw her was when she unexpectedly came to my place a week ago. She didn't say anything out of the ordinary, but she asked to borrow money. At the time, it didn't raise any red flags, but after you told me about those people who came to see you, my concern has skyrocketed," Aoife confessed, her mind racing back over the troubling series of events.

"How much did she borrow?" Nina asked.

"It's only three hundred euros, not even worth talking about," Aoife remarked, tapping her fingers on the table.

"Have you attempted to reach out to her host family or visited their home to see how she is?" Nina enquired while sipping her coffee.

"I visited their home a few days back, but nobody was there. I've only met them once before, and it was just a quick encounter. It happened on one of Laura's free days. When we arrived, Laura invited me inside, and I met her family. They stood in the living room. They were both polite to me but somewhat distant, their expressions reserved, and their smiles restrained. I figured their standoffish demeanour was just a cultural difference, assuming it was simply the French way," Aoife explained, recalling the encounter with a slight shrug.

"Listen, we need to find her, even if we're in over our heads," Aoife said, her voice carrying a sense of urgency as she looked around the bustling streets of Brussels. The city was a maze of cobblestone paths and towering buildings, each corner offering a new mystery. "I've only been in Brussels for a short time, just long enough to be enchanted by its charm but not enough to unravel its secrets. There are districts that remain unfamiliar, shadows I haven't explored yet. But perhaps there's someone who can assist us," she added, a hopeful smile spreading across her face, her eyes scanning the crowd for a friendly face or a possible ally.

Chapter 25

In Le Vigneron, a local wine bar with exposed brick walls, vintage wine racks, and low industrial lighting, Aoife and Nina enter with determined expressions and merge into the subdued hum of hushed conversations and soft jazz playing in the background. They navigate through the clustered tables to join Alex at a secluded corner where he sits with a glass of red wine, his eyes quietly alert as he senses the urgency of their arrival.

Aoife begins in an anxious voice, "Hello, thank you for meeting with us. By the way, this is Nina, also a friend of Laura's. Nina, meet Alex."

"Alex, we desperately need your help finding Laura," Nina insists with a voice that cuts through the air like a knife, laced with a fierce, unyielding urgency. The atmosphere crackles with intense determination and a palpable undercurrent of anxiety, foreshadowing the dangers ahead. They rely heavily on Alex's intimate knowledge of the city, their resolve steeling against the backdrop of clinking glasses and hushed conversations that fill the wine bar.

"OK, OK, both of you slow down. Start from the beginning," he suggested.

They both recounted the events of the past week or so and mentioned that they haven't been able to reach Laura. Still seated in the secluded corner, Alex sets his glass down with a deliberate clink and leans forward, his hand running slowly over the worn tabletop as he gathers his thoughts; his eyes flash with intensity as he shares his idea in a low, steady voice. "I know a guy who works at the local security firm which monitors our building, he can get us access to the surveillance footage from several key cameras around the neighbourhood. The last time I saw her was when I ran into her near the children's crèche, which is near my office," he explains, tapping a finger against the table to emphasise his plan.

Alex's posture straightens with determination, his back rigid and shoulders squared, while his intense gaze locks on both Aoife and Nina to convey his unwavering resolve. The soft lighting in the room casts gentle highlights across his face, accentuating the furrow of his brow and the seriousness of his expression as he meticulously outlines how the footage may capture Laura's sudden and frantic movements through darkened, shadowy alleys and past the imposing facade of the old, weathered bank building. Aoife leans in closer, her eyes widening slightly with intrigue and anticipation at the prospect of what Alex was describing. Nina nods slowly, her face thoughtful and contemplative, as she absorbs each detail with focused attention. Around them, the low murmur of nearby conversations blends harmoniously with the soft strains of smooth jazz wafting through the air, creating a backdrop of quiet ambiance as Alex continues to speak.

"If we can pinpoint the precise time and location where she might have been tracked, it could significantly narrow our search," he states, his hands weaving through the air with precise gestures that echo his calm yet urgent tone. His proposal serves as a crucial bridge between their desperate need to locate Laura and his practical connections within the local security network. As he outlines plans to contact his friend without delay, the group exchanges determined looks, their eyes reflecting a blend of cautious optimism and the gravity of their predicament. The room is charged with palpable tension; their body language, from subtle nods to the taut set of their shoulders, underscores the importance of this idea as a critical step in finding Laura.

The pair shifts their focus as Alex suggests, "We ought to delve into her au pair employers to unearth any potential discrepancies or hidden ties. Do either of you happen to know their names?" His voice carries a tone of curiosity and determination, eyes scanning his companions for any hint of recognition. The atmosphere is tense with the anticipation of discovery, and the dimly lit room seems to close in around them, urging them to unravel the mystery at hand.

Aoife snatches her phone with a determined grip, while Nina flicks open a compact leather notebook with precision. Alex adjusts his glasses, eyes narrowing as Aoife rapidly scrolls through a series of messages between herself and Laura on her phone trying to find the information he needs. The atmosphere crackles with intensity, a systematic calm underscored by an electrifying sense of urgency that demands immediate action.

Nina interjects, "Hold on, I recall Laura mentioning their first names; they're Camille and Pierre, and the children are Max and Chloe." As they continue to talk, their discussion is marked by meticulous planning.

"Aoife, perhaps you and Nina could gather more details about them from the crèche or the French class she attended," Alex proposes, taking a thoughtful sip of his beer, the frothy head leaving a trace on his upper lip. The pub around them buzzes with low conversations and clinking glasses as he continues, "It seems unlikely they'd send their kids to a crèche far from work. This might reveal a network extending beyond just their employment," he states, his eyes flicking between Aoife and Nina, gauging their reactions. The ambient lighting casts a warm glow over their table, creating a sense of camaraderie as they lean in to hear him over the murmur of the crowd.

As their investigative session intensifies, they divvy up tasks: Alex will connect with his contact at the security firm for more comprehensive surveillance, while Aoife and Nina will collect background information from local sources.

"We have to scrutinise every minute detail, no matter how deeply hidden, to track down Laura and halt whoever is hunting her. These are the only leads we have, and we cannot afford to fail," Nina declares with fierce determination.

"We're incredibly grateful, Alex. Honestly, we wouldn't know what to do without you," Aoife expresses, her voice filled with warmth and sincerity. She places her hand gently over his, her touch a silent but heartfelt gesture of appreciation. Her eyes meet his, conveying a depth of gratitude that words alone could not capture, before they part ways, each heading into the bustling world beyond.

Chapter 26

In the dim, muted light of a narrow alley, its walls adorned with vibrant and chaotic graffiti near a bustling metro station, Son stands tense and vigilant beside Laura. Together, the pair weaves through a labyrinth of flickering neon signs casting an eerie glow on the pavement and shadowy figures lurking in the periphery. Every passerby and each stealthy glance feels like the presence of a potential follower, while the distant wail of sirens and the low murmur of crowds create a symphony of tension that heightens his anxiety. His gaze darts rapidly from one shadowy entrance to the next, his mind racing with the silent consideration that any of these individuals might be part of the surveillance closing in on him and his companion. I boarded Line 1 at Montgomery, the map etched into my memory now from survival rather than sightseeing.

While waiting for the next train, Son recounts the terrifying moment when a mysterious attacker suddenly tried to kill him at the Delta Inc. office.

"I was burning the midnight oil at the office, as my role as an IT security specialist involves the crucial task of overseeing virus companies' data security and ensuring their files remain sealed under layers of encryption. During my routine checks, I stumbled upon some unsettling irregularities with a particular business. Their data, which should have been securely locked away, seemed to have been clandestinely copied by an external source. Alarm bells rang in my mind, so I immediately reported my findings to Harold Kemp, my supervisor. He leaned in, the gravity of the situation reflected in his stern gaze, and instructed me to keep this under wraps while I pursued a deeper investigation. As I peeled back the layers, I unearthed a troubling pattern—more companies were compromised. That's when I had to report this to my manager," he explained.

The fluorescent lights buzzed above the platform as Son described how the sudden intrusion broke the eerie silence of the nearly deserted workstations. Alone at his desk, he was writing an email to Harold Kemp:

If we don't lock down the ShadowStack portal, they'll keep pulling data through the backdoor for numerous corporations here and overseas. I've already flagged the behaviour, but it's getting ignored. I have no idea who authorised the Vanguard connection; it doesn't appear on any official records. This is unauthorised. I'll be escalating this further if IT doesn't take action.

Son hit the send button with a firm press, relishing the tactile feedback of the key under his finger. As the familiar electronic whoosh of the email departing his outbox resonated, the office door opened with a gentle creak.

"Initially, I dismissed the noise as the cleaning crew beginning their night shift. But when my eyes flicked up from my desk, I spotted a solitary figure slipping through the glass door. His gaze swept the room with a predatory intensity before he zeroed in on my workstation. Panic surged through me like electricity. Instinctively, I dropped into a crouch position, heart pounding in my chest, and snatched my laptop and backpack. Desperation fuelling my movements, I scrambled to my colleague's station two desks away, praying to remain unseen," he recounted, running trembling fingers through his now greasy hair.

"I tried to crawl quietly toward the door, ensuring I stayed hidden amidst the shadows, and frequently glancing back, my heart pounding, to check that he wasn't following me. As soon as I cautiously stood up and surveyed the dimly lit room, I noticed he was already rifling through the scattered papers on my desk, his back turned to me. It was my chance to make a break for it, but the door betrayed me with a drawn-out creak as I eased it open. I looked back in alarm and saw him swivelling toward me, his eyes locking onto mine, so I bolted, my footsteps echoing in the silence. The elevators were too risky, so I sprinted toward the stairwell, my breath quickening with each step. I realised, with a surge of panic, that he was only a few flights above me and closing in swiftly, so I darted onto the twelfth floor. I slipped into the dimly lit breakout room, the faint hum of the vending machine my only companion and concealed myself behind the small kitchenette. Moments later, he burst in after me, his footsteps heavy with determination. In a desperate bid for survival, I grabbed the nearest object—a toaster—and swung it with all my might, striking him on the head. He collapsed to the floor with a thud, and I seized the brief window of opportunity to escape before he could regain consciousness." Son looked up at me. My fingers fumbled.

In the aftermath of the attack, Son navigates the labyrinthine office corridors with precise determination, successfully evading the relentless stranger determined to eliminate him. Grabbing his worn backpack, which holds both his personal necessities and the stolen information, he slips out through a back exit into the uncertain embrace of a dark, rain-soaked city night.

A week after that fateful night, he found himself on a relentless run through the sprawling urban maze, driven by a palpable fear that lurks in every shadow. He darts from the cramped interiors of dingy motels to the crowded platforms of overfilled metro stations, his sweat-soaked jacket and trembling hands testifying to nights of sleepless anxiety. As he weaves through deserted alleys and dodges suspicious figures near shuttered storefronts, his every step is underscored by the urgency to stay one step ahead of his unseen pursuers—a desperate, adrenaline-fueled dance with danger that leaves him visibly shaken and perpetually vigilant.

"I made a copy of the data from my computer to a compact portable hard drive." The device felt cool and solid in my palm.

"You should keep a copy just in case something happens to me," he advised as the train pulled up to the station, his tone serious yet calm.

Chapter 27

The moment my eyes landed on the motel, I recognised it as one of those seedy establishments that reek of mildew and poor decisions, perched on the city's outskirts like a jagged, decaying tooth. The neon sign flickered ominously, casting a sickly glow over the peeling paint and cracked windows. Despite the unsettling vibe, my body protested fiercely—my legs felt like lead, and my head throbbed with a relentless intensity. I no longer possessed the energy to argue my way out of the situation. Son took charge, as he always did, with his quiet, efficient manner that was as unreadable as a closed book. His calm demeanour grated on my nerves, as if he were detached from the gravity of our situation. It was as though we were merely two casual tourists lost in the labyrinthine streets of Brussels, rather than two individuals desperately evading those who pursued us.

He requested two separate rooms, "Just in case," he'd explain. As if physical space between us could protect us when things turned sour. Yet, I allowed him to handle it. I couldn't bear to think any longer; I just needed a door to close and a private place to break down.

The corridor was steeped in the pungent odour of stale tobacco, mingling with the heavy scent of damp, musty carpet, creating an almost suffocating atmosphere. The air felt thick as I walked through, and I clenched the cold metal key in my hand with such intensity that its jagged edges pressed deeply into my skin, leaving behind a series of distinct, reddened imprints.

Son paused at his door. "Get some rest," he suggested, as if everything was fine. As if we weren't teetering on the brink of disaster.

I hesitated, then looked up at him. "Do you mind if I borrow your laptop? Just for a bit."

He turned slightly, gave me a quick glance. "You looking something up?"

"Just... trying to connect a few dots," I said, not quite ready to explain.

He didn't ask. Just nodded once and pulled the laptop from the side pocket of his duffel. "Go ahead," he said, handing it over. "It's clean. No one's tracking this."

"Thanks," I murmured.

The key twisted in the lock with a grating, sticky resistance, each turn scraping like metal grinding on metal. When the door finally gave way, it creaked open to reveal a room that offered little comfort.

It was dimly lit, the walls stained and close, as if pressing inward. The air hung heavy with the scent of neglect—dust rising in lazy spirals through the thin, filtered light.

I stepped inside, dropped my bag by the wall, and sat heavily on the edge of the bed, the mattress groaning beneath me. My hands still trembled faintly, the adrenaline refusing to fully release its grip. The lid of the laptop was cool to the touch. I opened it slowly, as though the contents might explode in my face.

The screen blinked on, flooding the room with sterile, blue-white light. I adjusted the angle and pulled my knees up slightly, balancing the device as I waited for the desktop to load.

My reflection hovered ghost-like on the black screen for a moment before it vanished. The browser opened with a quiet click. My fingers hovered above the keys. I hesitated, heart pounding, then placed them lightly on the keyboard.

The cursor blinked, patient and expectant.

I typed: *Erin Blake Brussels* and hit enter.

Links loaded slowly—news blurbs, scattered mentions on Reddit, a missing persons database entry. I clicked none of them.

Instead, I opened Instagram in a separate tab, my stomach tightening as I typed her name again: @erinb.can.

Her profile appeared almost instantly. Still public. Still active—technically.
Even though I knew dozens of people had probably looked her up, scrolled through her posts, dissected every photo and comment, I needed to see it for myself. Not as a headline. Not through someone else's theory.

The profile picture was the same I remembered from the flyer at the Alliance Française: Erin smiling into the sun, her hair caught in the breeze, eyes crinkled with unassuming joy.

Her bio read:
Canadian in Brussels
Au pair life | waffles

I scrolled through her feed, each photo a frozen fragment of a life that seemed deceptively ordinary. There was a post from Grand Place, lit up at night. Another of her holding a cone of frites with a cheeky grin. She had the kind of face that made you believe she'd never needed to worry about anything.

Then came the image that stopped me cold.

A mirror selfie in what looked like a marbled corridor—opulent, cold, expensive.

"Host family's place is a castle"
Tagged: #cipherion #ucclelife #brusselsliving

I sat back slowly, pulse pounding so hard it echoed in my ears, drowning out the clatter of cutlery and the hum of conversation around me. My grip tightened around the edge of the table, knuckles whitening. Where do I know that name from? The thought sparked like electricity behind my eyes. My chest constricted.

Then it hit me.

#Cipherion - Pierre's company. The name I'd seen buried in that encrypted folder, the one I wasn't meant to open, the one I wasn't even supposed to know existed. The logo had flashed briefly across the screen before I closed it, thinking I'd imagined it. But I didn't.

A tremor moved through my fingers. My throat dried instantly, and I shifted in my seat, suddenly aware of how exposed I felt. The café's warmth pressed in around me, suffocating instead of comforting.

It was like the walls had narrowed, the sounds too loud, the light too bright. I tried to slow my breathing, but a coil of dread had already wrapped itself tight around my ribs.

They were connected. Somehow, they were all connected.

And I was sitting in the middle of it.

The deeper I scrolled, the more the captions shifted. The tone light-hearted at first, then trailing into shorter, vaguer remarks.

Her final post was dated nearly three weeks ago: a close-up of a coffee cup, a leather-bound notebook half in frame.

Caption: "Rainy days and secrets."
Location tag: Café Kalima

I clicked open the comments. Most were harmless—emojis, friendly replies, jokes about the weather.

But three stood out.

@sydb09: you okay?
@caroblake: please call me. we're getting worried.

@mimifries: anyone else heard from her??

That one had a like. Just one.

From a private account with no profile picture.

A chill rippled across my skin, something's off about this whole disappearance.

I clicked on the account that liked the comment. No posts. No bio. Just a handle: @watching.erin.

My hand moved off the trackpad slowly, like I'd just touched something sharp.

Curiosity tightening into unease, I opened a new tab and typed "Cipherion Global" into the search bar. Within seconds, headlines and polished press releases filled the screen—sleek branding, buzzwords like predictive analytics, behavioral insight, data sovereignty.

It all looked harmless enough at first. Sterile. Clinical. The kind of company that boasted about "reshaping digital governance" and "enabling secure intelligence for tomorrow."

But buried beneath the surface-level polish were links that felt colder. Darker.

I clicked one.
Cipherion Global: The Quiet Giant Behind Europe's Data Watchdogs. One file stood out: 'CleanupProtocol_04.'

Another:
Outsourcing Oversight – How Private Surveillance Firms Like Cipherion Are Shaping National Security Policy.

My pulse picked up. The deeper I dug, the more disturbing the pattern became. Cipherion wasn't just analyzing public data—they were contracting directly with governments, creating AI-driven models for crowd behavior, protest forecasting, political sentiment tracking.

I stared at the screen, a cold weight settled in my stomach.

This wasn't just a company my employer worked for.

This was a machine that thrived on knowing too much.

And Erin Blake had tagged their name in a photo like it was nothing.

I scrolled back to her post. "Host family's place is a castle □"—the opulent hallway. The Cipherion hashtag. She must have lived with someone high up.

I rubbed a hand over my face and leaned back against the headboard, the laptop still warm against my legs.

Chapter 28

I snapped the laptop shut, the sharp click slicing through the room's silence like a warning. What I'd uncovered settled over me with crushing weight, pressing into my chest until it felt hard to breathe. I was still in the same clothes I'd worn through the chaos—the chase, the fear, the unravelling—and every part of me throbbed with exhaustion I'd been too wired to notice until now. My fingers fumbled. I wasn't trained for this, I was improvising with every breath.

I let myself fall backward onto the bed, barely managing to toe off my shoes. The mattress sagged beneath me, its rough fabric scraping against my skin, a dull reminder that I hadn't even made it under the covers. My body gave up before my mind could catch up. The pillow met the side of my face, and I sank instantly, thoughts dissolving, breath slowing. No dreams came. Just darkness—heavy, thick, and absolute.

It felt as if I had been enveloped in the depths of sleep for hours when an unexpected sound from the room next door shattered the silence, jolting me awake and disrupting the serene cocoon of my slumber. The noise was sharp and sudden, like a clap of thunder in the stillness of night. My heart pounded in my chest as I lay there, trying to discern what had disturbed the peace. Just as I was about to rise and open the door, ready to confront whatever lay beyond, I heard it again, a soft, yet unmistakable whisper of movement that sent a shiver down my spine outside.

The piercing click shattered the oppressive silence—a sound that would forever claw at the edges of my sanity like a relentless predator. My hands shook violently, betraying my terror as I painstakingly opened the door. There he was—not Son, but him. A menacing stranger loomed in the dimly lit hallway, his hood drawn low, casting sinister shadows that devoured his features. The gun he held was rock-steady, aimed with a terrifying precision that sent a frigid avalanche through my veins, freezing every drop of blood. He was a dark spectre, the living embodiment of my most dreaded nightmares, wrenched from the shadows to stand before me. My mouth gaped open in a silent scream, lodged painfully in my throat, suffocated by a relentless, paralysing fear. He turned just in time to lock eyes with me, sealing my fate in that soul-crushing gaze.

"Qu'est-ce que tout ce bruit que nous entendons? Nous essayons de dormir." The voice, tinged with frustration, emerged from a woman a few rooms away. She stood in the dimly lit doorway, her hair tousled from sleep, with shadows casting across her face. The noise had roused her from her slumber, and she peered into the hallway, eyes narrowed, trying to discern the source of the disturbance that pierced the night's silence.

The man stood resolute, emanating an aura of formidable composure. His eyes bore into mine with a piercing intensity, as if he were dissecting my very essence to confirm a crucial truth or ascertain an identity of paramount importance. Then, with unwavering determination, he pivoted sharply and marched away with a commanding confidence. His demeanour was a calculated calm, oozing an assured nonchalance, as if he had just executed a mission of life-altering significance.

I gasped, my breath catching hard in my throat as a wave of panic surged through me. My hand shook as I reached for Sol's door—it was already ajar, hanging just enough to make it feel wrong, like something was off. I pushed it open slowly, my fingers numb. My fingers fumbled. I wasn't trained for this; I was improvising with every breath.

The room was still. Too still. He lay across the bed at an odd angle; his body twisted slightly like he'd fallen and never moved again. One arm dangled off the side, the other tucked under him. Blood had pooled beneath his head and soaked into the pillow, a deep red stain spreading across the sheets. The wound on his temple was sharp and brutal, there was no mistaking what had happened.

My legs nearly gave out. I grabbed the doorframe to steady myself, heart pounding so hard I thought it might tear through my chest. The air felt heavy, like it hadn't moved in hours. The quiet buzz of a nearby lamp was the only sound in the room.

I couldn't look away.

It felt like the world had cracked open—and I'd stepped straight into the heart of something I couldn't undo.

My legs buckled beneath me, unable to support the weight of my shock and anguish, and I crashed to the floor, the world around me dissolving into a chaotic blur of sound and colour. The room seemed to spin, a dizzying vortex of grief and disbelief. With a voice raw and frantic, I screamed his name over and over, as if sheer willpower and desperation could turn back the clock, rekindle the life so cruelly snatched from his motionless body. But his eyes, once vibrant and full of life, now stared blankly, hollow and lifeless, their light snuffed out, leaving behind a deafening silence that crushed my soul with its weight. The air was thick with the metallic scent of blood and the suffocating presence of loss. And that's when the horrifying truth slammed into me with the force of a tempest. We were never safe. Not for a single minute.

Chapter 29

I grabbed what I could from the motel, including his laptop and suddenly found myself wandering along the deserted streets. Seeking clarity, I stumbled upon a quaint café that had just started baking fresh bread, filling the air with a wonderful aroma. Needing a moment to think, I decided to go inside and ordered a coffee, using Son's wallet, which I had taken from his room along with his backpack. I grabbed my phone and browsed through my contacts, eager to reach out to someone, anyone, a friend, but I hesitated, not wanting to put them at risk. I found Aoife's number and was about to dial it, but then I thought better of it.

I yanked the folder from Son's backpack, the weight of his relentless investigative efforts palpable in my grip. As I rifled through the meticulously organised pages crammed with business names and addresses reported to Harold Kemp, the bakery's soft hum swelled around me, laced with the intoxicating scent of freshly baked bread and pastries. Suddenly, one business name screamed off the page, its letters burning into my mind, igniting a fierce sense of recognition. It clawed insistently at the edges of my memory, like an earworm melody on the tip of my tongue, yet the exact encounter remained maddeningly elusive.

"Wow, Longreach Logistics," I whispered to myself. The name struck a chord—I knew this company, and it was where Alex worked! I hesitated for a moment, recalling the business card he had given me with his direct number boldly printed on it. My mind was torn between curiosity and apprehension. With a mix of eagerness and uncertainty, I slowly typed his mobile number into my phone, my fingers hovering over the screen before finally pressing the call button.

"Shit, he's not picking up." I sighed and hung up. The clock was inching closer to eight in the morning, and a gentle urgency crept into my movements. I quickly collected my belongings, the chair scraping slightly against the tiled floor as I stood. The café was filled with the comforting aroma of freshly brewed coffee and the soft murmur of morning chatter. With a final glance at the corner I was leaving behind, I stepped outside into the crisp morning air. The sunlight was just beginning to cast its warm glow over the city, and with purposeful strides, I set off towards his workplace, the bustling streets gradually coming to life around me.

The journey to the European Union district stretched on for over an hour, allowing me ample time to become absorbed in my own thoughts. Seated comfortably yet restlessly in the carriage, I tried once more to place a call, only to be met with the familiar monotone of voicemail. As the train drew closer to the district, the atmosphere shifted and the carriage became a bustling hive of activity. The aisles, once open and spacious, were now filled with a sea of passengers standing shoulder to shoulder, their murmurs and movements creating a soft cacophony that pulsed through the air.

Finally, the train pulled into Schuman Station, its brakes screeching softly as it came to a halt, sparking a wave of movement as passengers poured out of the carriages. I merged into the bustling crowd, yet my mind was already darting ahead, picturing myself climbing the wide, stone steps toward the sleek Rue de la Loi. There it was—a glass-panelled entrance of the design office where he worked.

When I arrived at the building, the typical morning hustle and bustle was in full swing, with a small café on the ground floor serving staff their morning caffeine fix. I made my way through the lobby toward the information desk, aware of the security guard's watchful eyes. Longreach Logistics occupied five floors, from the eighth to the thirteenth. Unsure of which floor he was on, I figured the smartest approach was to go to the reception on the eighth floor and enquire about him there.

The elevator door slid open, and I stepped inside, pressing the button for the eighth floor. I couldn't help but notice that the other passengers in the elevator gave me odd looks, probably because my jeans and long-sleeve shirt didn't exactly scream corporate attire. The bell rang on the elevator announcing level eight, I walked out to the reception desk that greeted me. The lights were on, but the front desk was empty, no receptionist. The office upstairs buzzed with conversation as everyone got on with their tasks, accompanied by the gentle hum of the air conditioning starting up for the day.

The sign on the desk read: "If the reception desk is unattended ring the bell."

So that's precisely what I did and waited. In less than a minute, a young woman with flowing blonde hair emerged gracefully from the back room. Her hair caught the light, shimmering like strands of gold as she moved with a subtle elegance.

"Hi, can I help you?" she enquired, as she eyed me from head to toe.

"I hope so, I'm wanting to speak with Alex De Smet," I answered.

"Do you have an appointment?" she asked, flipping through her calendar.

"Not exactly, but I'm a good friend of his and just need a quick moment with him. Could you please tell him Laura is here?" I asked.

"Take a seat and I'll see what I can do," she said as she gestured me to the lounge opposite her desk. She was already on the phone when I took a seat.

"Yes, I have a visitor here for Mr. De Smet." She glanced up at me briefly, then away, listening.

A pause. Then, her eyebrows lifted just slightly. Not in surprise, exactly, more like quiet confirmation. She turned slightly in her seat, voice lowering a notch.

"I understand... No, his calendar is empty for today and the upcoming week as well. Okay, I'll inform her." She placed the receiver back with deliberate, practised ease. Her hands rested gently in front of her keyboard, and she turned to me, fully composed and professional, but there was a hint of uncertainty in her eyes.

"I'm sorry, Mr. De Smet isn't in the office today." The words landed softly, but their weight was immediate.

I blinked, noticing my mouth open a bit as if he was about to respond, but what would he say? "Are you certain?: Naturally, she was certain. Receptionists in such establishments were not prone to speculation.

"He didn't say anything?" I asked finally, trying to keep my voice even.

"No," the woman replied, with a sympathetic tilt of her head. "From what I understand, he left town yesterday on a personal matter. It was unexpected."

Unexpected.

That word echoed, louder than it should have.

"Right," I murmured, offering a slight nod. I didn't really feel it. "Okay. Thanks." I flashed her a polite smile, the sort that signals the end of a conversation rather than the start of a new one.

I pivoted slowly, moving away from the desk with careful steps, as if trying not to disrupt a room that had just transformed. The city beyond the glass seemed a bit farther away now.

Chapter 30

I barely had a second to strategise my next move when a text message from Victor slammed into my inbox, blunt and unmistakable.

Meet me ASAP, I have important information about Pierre.

My hand trembled violently as I read the words, each letter throbbing with a relentless urgency. My mind raced, a chaotic storm of thoughts and possibilities crashing together as I struggled to grasp the full weight of Victor's terse yet urgent note.

I fixed my eyes on the screen, my gaze unwavering as I blinked rapidly to clear the blur. The text lay there, sharp and unyielding like a jagged stone, its edges cutting into my consciousness. I read it once more, my breath hitching in quick, shallow bursts, each inhale sharp and urgent. My pulse raced erratically, a wild drumbeat echoing in my ears, as anxiety gripped me with a cold, unrelenting hold.

Grey clouds hung low over the streets of Brussels. Rain loomed on the horizon, threatening yet not yet arriving. It felt as if the entire world was holding its breath. I had expected to feel relieved to hear from him, but something in the message scratched at the edge of my thoughts, leaving me uneasy. The phone vibrated insistently in my hand. I swallowed hard and tapped the screen.

"Hello?"

"Laura," Victor spoke quickly and abruptly. "We need to meet tonight, it's regarding Pierre. His work, the people he's connected with—"

I interrupted him. "I don't get it. Why are you telling me this?"

There was a pause. I pictured him back in his house on the outskirts of Brussels, surrounded by books and maps, piecing together the fragments of a puzzle.

"You have to trust me. There's no one else. We need to talk before it's too late."

My mind stumbled over the words. "They killed Son, how do I know it's safe?"

His tone dropped lower, laden with urgency. "We can't speak on the phone. There are ears everywhere."

I hesitated. I'd been careful, staying off the radar. Was this a trap? A ploy to lure me back in? I sensed him take a breath, the impatience in his voice barely concealed.

"Seven o'clock tomorrow morning," he said. "Leopold Park. By the lake. I'll find you."

Then, a click and he was gone. The silence filled the void again, stretching wide and deep. I rested my forehead against the window, closing my eyes. I thought back to the last time I saw Victor, those sharp grey eyes behind his glasses urging me to get out while I could. The weight of this new information settled over me, pressing down and making it hard to breathe. My fingers fumbled. I wasn't trained for this, I was improvising with every breath.

Information about Pierre. So many troubling possibilities radiated from that one phrase. He might be back in Paris, perhaps even Brussels. Could he have discovered my location? Is that why Victor reached out? I pressed my fingers to my temples, trying to clear the muddled thoughts as I spent the next few hours in a restless daze pacing, checking the clock, listening for phantom footsteps outside the door.

The park soon loomed ahead, its bare trees standing like skeletal sentinels against the morning sky. I glanced behind me more than once, half-expecting to see a shadowy figure in pursuit. The lake lay dark and still, a mirror catching the faint light from the distant city. I came to a stop at the water's edge, my heart pounding as my thoughts tumbled into a frantic race: Victor, Pierre, the ever-present sense of danger. My breath clouded in the cool air as I waited, alone and exposed.

I arrived much earlier than needed, with no one else around. The silence enveloped me like a heavy cloak, and I tightened my coat against the chill, questioning my decision to be there.

Through the morning fog, I saw Victor approaching, but he wasn't alone; Camille was with him.

"Hello, Laura," Camille greeted as she drew nearer.

"I hear you've been caught up in quite the whirlwind of drama these past few days," she said with a playful smile, her eyes twinkling with curiosity and a hint of amusement.

Victor nods, glancing around the surroundings. "Wanted to make sure it was safe."

She gives a small, knowing smile. "Is it ever?"

They fall into silence, not awkward but deliberate. Camille lets it stretch, watching the flicker of concern on Victor's face.

"Do you believe Pierre was responsible for Son's death?" I eventually enquire.

Victor pushes his glasses up aggressively, his eyes blazing with certainty. "I'm absolutely sure it was him," he insists, his voice a low growl. "The data breach unmistakably bears his signature, and he and his associates will stop at nothing—absolutely nothing—to get what they want back."

Camille leans back, crossing her arms. "He's become sloppy then."

Victor shakes his head. "Sloppy, or overconfident. Or both.

Either way, he thinks you're on his side."

"He's not entirely wrong," she says, the ghost of a grin playing at her lips.

She holds his gaze, allowing the truth of his words to hang between them. Camille feels a pulse of satisfaction at her own foresight.

"The breach will bring others in. We may lose control."

Victor slowly and deliberately sits down on the bench facing the lake.

"We need to act now, before it happens," he says, folding his arms.

"Do you trust this young lady?" Victor asks Camille while looking directly at me.

"I must," Camille replies, her voice carrying a tone of resignation, acknowledging the fragility of their situation. "She's innocent, merely caught in the wrong place at the wrong time."

"You can say that again," I blurted out.

Camille nods, pondering the complexities of their scheme. The threads are fragile, some so thin they're almost undetectable. One misstep, one misplaced trust, and everything could fall apart. Camille speaks once more, her voice so soft that only Victor and I can hear her.

"So can we use this to our advantage? Get her to convince Pierre that she can be trusted and set a trap?"

Victor's expression is unreadable, a flicker of something like doubt passing across his eyes.

"What if it fails?"

Victor considers. "That's the gamble. But it will give us the chance we need."

"And if not?" Camille says, her gaze turning steely. "If he catches on?"

Victor's face tightens, and the lines of worry cut deep. "Then he'll wish he hadn't."

The edge in his voice is unmistakable, slicing through the air with quiet force. Camille doesn't respond. Instead, she lowers herself onto the damp bench, the chill seeping through her clothes. They find themselves all alone, free from attachments, yet there's empowerment in that solitude. It allows them to act outside the bounds of family ties or loyalty. Victor pulls a small envelope from his coat.

"For you," Victor says. "To make things easier; what you need to do is in that. Read it when we are gone."

"Hold on," I said sharply, my voice cutting through the air. I didn't move, didn't reach for the envelope sitting on the table between us. My hands stayed firmly in my lap, clenched tight. "I never agreed to this. Not once."

I looked up, meeting their eyes with a cold, steady stare.

"Did it ever even occur to you to ask if I wanted to be involved? Or was I just convenient? Just someone to pull into this mess without a second thought, you don't get to decide this for me," I said, quieter now, but with more force. Not after everything. You don't get to drag me in and act like it was always part of the plan."

The envelope sat there like it might burn me if I touched it.

"Listen to me, Laura, you don't have a choice," Camille cut in, her voice low but crackling with urgency. "This isn't a negotiation."

I froze.

"Your friends are in serious danger. Son's dead, murdered in cold blood. And there's a price on your head," she said, each word hitting like a slap. "These people? They don't care who they hurt. They don't stop. Ever."

Her eyes locked onto mine, fierce and unflinching. "Do you understand? This is real. Right now, it's not about what you want—it's about staying alive."

Camille was right; I found myself backed into a corner with no options, no matter how many angles I tried to view the situation from. The weight of my predicament settled heavily on my shoulders, leaving me with little choice. With a reluctant sigh, I reached out for the envelope, its crisp edges cool against my fingertips. I carefully tucked it into my bag, the paper rustling softly as it nestled among my belongings, a tangible reminder of the decision I was compelled to make.

They lapse into silence once more, the weight of what they've shared pressing heavily around them. Victor seems to retreat into himself, and Camille realises this is how he must spend most of his days, sheltered in the shadow, trying to protect her children, alone with his thoughts and the dangers he cannot escape. She shifts and leans forward.

"We are doing the right thing," she says, not sure if she is reassuring him or herself.

Victor meets her eyes. "As long as we're breathing, yes."

Camille stands up from the park bench. "Then let's keep it that way."

Victor nods, once, an acknowledgment and a dismissal. Camille turns and leaves, her coat trailing behind her like a whisper of intent.

I hover for a moment beside the bench, unsure if there's more to say. The rain has slowed to a drizzle, but the air still carries that electric weight of something unfinished.

"You'll be okay?" I ask, my voice low.

Victor doesn't look at me. "Does it matter?"

I hesitate. "It does to me."

That gets his attention. He turns just slightly, his expression unreadable. "Then keep moving. Don't look back."

I nodded. It's all I can do.

I step away, crossing toward a nearby tree for shelter as cars rush past, their headlights slicing through the gloom. My coat clings to my back, damp with rain and tension. I push a strand of wet hair from my face, steal one last glance at the bench—and then I vanish into the growing dark, just another shadow swallowed by Brussels.

The rain has eased, yet the sky remains burdened with thick grey clouds ready to burst. I stop under a nearby tree for cover, observing as cars speed by, their headlights cutting through the early evening gloom. My mind races, piecing together more details, planning the next steps. I tuck a loose strand of hair behind my ear, adjust my coat, and vanish into the waning light. My figure blends into the cityscape, becoming just another form among countless others.

Victor remains seated alone on the bench, his back curved and shoulders tense. He watches as I gradually fade into the shadows.

Chapter 31

I come across a run-down motel just off a quiet side street, tucked between a shuttered bakery and a boarded-up laundromat. Its flickering neon sign buzzed faintly in the rain, casting a dull pink glow onto the cracked pavement. The lobby was empty, no music, no conversation, just the low hum of an old vending machine and the faint tick of a wall clock that hadn't kept proper time in years. The man at the front desk barely looked up as I signed in under a false name and paid in cash. No questions. Just a sliding of keys across a chipped counter and a nod toward the staircase.

I let myself into a second-floor room that smelled faintly of damp carpet and stale air freshener. The walls were yellowing at the corners, and the light above the bed buzzed with an uneven flicker. Still, it was quiet. Anonymous. Safe enough for now.

I dropped my bag on the faded floral armchair in the corner and sat down at the small wooden table by the window, the glass streaked with rain. Perfect.

With trembling hands, I grasp the crisp, white envelope, hesitating for a moment before finally breaking the seal with a soft, satisfying crackle. My eyes scan the instructions twice, absorbing each word as if it were a lifeline. Carefully, I fold the letter along its creases, slide it back into the envelope, and place it gently aside on the polished wooden table. Beside it sits a neat stack of fifty-euro notes, their edges perfectly aligned and gleaming under the soft light. I quickly thumb through the bills, their smooth texture brushing against my fingertips, and estimate the sum to be an impressive total of a thousand euros resting in my hands. I realised that having options was now a possibility. As I picked up the envelope once more, ready to open it, the sound of footsteps outside the door caught my attention. The footsteps hesitated briefly before continuing. I remained perfectly still, waiting until I was certain I was alone again.

The air in the motel is stale. Everything smells like yesterday's coffee. The lone bulb in the kitchen hums overhead, I check the window again (my paranoia getting the better of me) but no one is down there either. Only rain and parked cars in front of the motel.

The letter lacks a signature, yet I instantly identify it as Victor's handwriting. The neat, looping script clearly explains how to infiltrate Pierre's network, evade detection, and navigate the system's vulnerabilities. I take a deep breath and release it slowly. I should have anticipated this when Pierre began his enquiries; I should have known. He is aware that I've seen the confidential documents Son duplicated, or at the very least, he's heard rumours. Victor likely knows as well; he's probably heard everything. This explains the letter's precision and straightforwardness. However, there's no way to determine how he discovered it, who else might be aware, or if it's already too late as I refold the letter and tuck it back into the envelope.

My mind flits to Pierre. His cold, calculating eyes. His casual cruelty, like he doesn't even know he's doing it. The threat he represents looms large and dangerous. These instructions must be right. They must be perfect. A slip means he finds her. A slip means it's over.

I gazed at the phone and powered it on, revealing a screen crowded with missed calls and texts. They seemed anxious, nearly desperate, yet I disregard them. With a steady hand, I enter Pierre's number. The message is audacious, nearly daring. He'll understand its gravity.

I begin to type: -

"You know what I found. I'm not trying to blow this up, but I need to be safe. Proof of what you did is on this drive. I want out. No cops. If I disappear, it goes wide. Downloading it triggers a trace. Want to

talk. Laura"

The words spilled out quickly and angrily, a defiant pushback against my fear. My heart races like an alarm. I can't make a mistake. It can't come across as a bluff. The unyielding surge of adrenaline heightens my concentration. I press send, experiencing a fleeting relief, a deceptive sense of control in a chaotic world, though it feels like it's scorching my hand. For a moment, I considered smashing it and fleeing. But I knew that the only way through this was to face it head-on. My finger lingers over the power button. The battery is nearly drained, so I hastily plug it into the power point. I should have charged it, should have been more prepared.

Missed call. Missed call. Missed call. My thumb swiftly brushes past them, indifferent. There are messages as well, coming in nonstop. Call me, what's happening? I bit my lip hard, my heart racing with the urgency. I skip to the most recent one: This isn't a game, Laura, Aoife explains. I couldn't resist a laugh, a brief, breathless chuckle. As if they have any idea what's really going on.

My mind is a tempest of thoughts about Pierre, shoving everything else into the background. This moment feels crucial. I need to be clever, to convey just how serious I am about this. Yet, a wave of panic crashes over me. What if he's already ahead, closing in on me? I can't afford to lose focus now. I gulp down a deep breath, desperately seeking some calm amidst the chaos. My fingers fumbled. I wasn't trained for this, I was improvising with every breath.

The next words seem daunting: There's proof of what you did on this drive. My thumb wavers above the keys. I crave an escape. No police. But what if he doesn't take the bait? And what if he does? My mind spirals through the possibilities, each fraught with risk. Still, I can't let it stop me; if there's even a chance I vanish, the data will go public. My mouth is parched, but the urgency is overpowering, and the potential fallout no longer fazes me.

The phone's screen dims as I switch it off. Silence returns, and I fling it into my bag, hoping distance might offer protection. A frantic calm, an unexpected sense of control, washes over me. He has to understand how serious I am. He must. I swallow hard, my chest constricting with a mix of hope and dread.

A faint buzzing sound starts up—electric, low. For a heartbeat, I think it's in my head. Then I realise: the ancient fridge in the corner has kicked back to life, rattling with the same uncertain rhythm as my thoughts. I glance toward it, irrationally wondering if I should unplug it, just to kill the noise. But the stillness that follows only sharpens the edges of my nerves.

The room smells faintly of mildew and stale soap. I pace to the narrow window and draw the curtain back an inch. Nothing but the parking lot: a cracked stretch of concrete under the dim sodium glow of the motel's lone streetlamp. Still, I step back and let the curtain fall into place. I perch on the edge of the bed again, this time careful to keep my bag close. The drive is inside it. The evidence. My insurance policy and my threat, all in one small device. I wonder if he's read the message already. If his pulse spiked the way mine did when I pressed "send".

My hands itch with nervous energy, but there's nothing left to do. I've set the trap. Now I have to wait.

The wait is unbearable.

I pick up the glass of water I filled earlier from the chipped bathroom tap. It tastes metallic, but I force a few gulps down. The silence creeps back in—dense, cloying. No sirens. No footsteps. Just that awful fridge again, clicking and humming like it might give out any second.

I check the clock. Only four minutes have passed.

Gripping the edge of the mattress, I force my breathing to slow. He has to know I'm not bluffing. That if I disappear, the contents of that drive will hit the right inboxes—journalists, the encrypted cloud folder Alex helped me set up, the auto-email chain Pierre doesn't know exists.

But still. What if he calls my bluff?

I lie back, staring at the cracked ceiling paint, willing them to hold the answers I don't have. The fear is still there, of course, but it's sharper now, refined into something colder, quieter. A resolve.

Whatever happens, I'm not running again.

Chapter 32

In less than an hour, Pierre replied to me with a message:

"We can resolve this. There's no need for anyone else to get involved. Just tell me what you want, and we can make this disappear, you have my word."

His words, though trying to assert control and secure silence, subtly revealed a note of desperation, highlighting his determination to keep his illegal activities under wraps no matter what the cost.

I anticipated his response, yet I wasn't ready to see his message.

I dropped the phone onto the bedside table, my breath catching in my throat. The audacity of it. The absolute nerve, he knows that I want my life back. My heart pounds, echoing in the hollow space of the room. Safety and distance. That's what I want. What I need. But this, this is nothing more than an attempt to shut me up, did he mean to make me disappear?

I picked up the phone and type.

"I'm not asking twice—if anything happens to me, that file gets out. The choice is yours."

The words slam onto the screen with a relentless fury.

My finger hovers over the send button, hesitating. But not for long. I fire it off, watching as the message vanishes into the ether. The tension stretches, the silence in the room almost unbearable as I wait for his next move. For whatever comes next.

No reply!

The phone vibrates again, but I don't rush back to it. Not this time. Let him wait. Let him stew. I've already told him what I want. Now it's up to him to decide what happens next. It's his move. But I'm ready for it, no matter what he thinks he can do. No matter how he thinks he can control this.

I pick up the phone and read his reply.

"It's a simple swap, give me the data and you'll get your life back. Today, four o'clock sharp at the Pont de Buda bridge, right by the EU offices. Make sure you're alone and for your own sake, don't be late."

I glanced at the clock, its hands ticking relentlessly forward. The minute hand had just landed firmly on number twelve, marking the hour as two o'clock. A sense of urgency washed over me, realising that the afternoon had slipped away faster than anticipated. My mind raced, searching for a solution, but the dwindling hours left me with barely enough time to devise any sort of plan.

The European Union offices were conveniently accessible via the one and five metro lines. I disembarked at the bustling Schuman Station, a junction for both lines, and ascended into daylight onto Rue de la Loi. The street, framed by towering buildings, was beginning to swell with a stream of people concluding their workday, their footsteps creating a rhythmic beat against the pavement. Despite the growing crowd, the avenue remained passable. I navigated through the throng, guided by the clear, blue signs that pointed the way, until I reached the tranquil canal, where the elegant curves of Pont de Buda gracefully arched over the shimmering water.

I stepped onto the bridge, watching the water move below me, and stopped halfway, just where the iron rail dipped slightly from years of weight. People passed behind me: commuters, couples, someone on a bike with music leaking from their earphones. None of them mattered. What mattered was who might come next. I closed my hand around the phone in my coat pocket. No new messages from Pierre. He said he'd be here.

I struggled to piece together his face, the details slipping away like a dream upon waking. The sharp angles and features now a smeared canvas, blurred by time like a painting ravaged by relentless rain. Yet, his voice lingered in my memory, vivid and piercing. The way he said my name with venom, the calculated pause before he wove a lie.

At the far end of the bridge, a man stood as still as a statue, his silhouette starkly defined against the dimming sky. He was cloaked in a long, ominous black coat that seemed to absorb the fading light around him, casting an air of mystery and foreboding. The coat billowed slightly in the chilling breeze, adding to the enigmatic aura that surrounded him.

He was motionless, as if waiting for some unspoken command. Was it him? A sense of dread clawed at me, and I shifted my weight uneasily, turning my face slightly to the side, desperate to remain unseen. The wind, sharp and cold, tugged insistently at my scarf as I stared down at the river, where the fractured reflections of light danced erratically like shattered glass.

Then, another figure emerged, cutting through the scene with vibrant defiance, a girl with a striking red umbrella. She glided past the man without hesitation. He remained unyielding, and she walked on, unperturbed by his presence, towards me. I barely noticed her because my attention was focused on the man who was staring at me.

"Laura, listen carefully and follow my instructions. We're running out of time," the girl insisted, pausing to fix her gaze on me.

I was stunned. "Aoife, is that really you?"

"Are you alright?" she enquired, her voice steady and composed, though the subtle quiver at its edges hinted at her underlying concern. Her eyes, however, told a different story; they were deep pools of emotion that shimmered with worry and compassion, betraying the facade of calmness she struggled to maintain.

"I thought I was ready, but then I saw you," I blurted out, my voice shaking with urgency. "What happened? How on earth did you get pulled into this mess?"

"They have Nina," Aoife's voice wavered as she spoke the last word. She stepped closer, her voice dropping to a whisper as if the walls had ears. "And they won't release her. Not unless you follow their instructions to the letter."

A car roared by at the street's end, shattering the thick silence that hung heavily between us. Its headlights sliced through the darkness, casting two piercing beams of light that flooded over both of them, illuminating the tension in stark relief.

With a raw throat, I asked her, "What do they want?"

Aoife paused, glancing away.

Chapter 33

"All they want is the drive and any copies you got from Son before he died," her voice trembled, barely a whisper as fear gripped her, the unspoken terror that Nina might meet the same grim fate hanging heavily in the air.

"Laura, we both desperately need Nina back safely, don't we? Then, listen closely and don't miss a word," Aoife commanded, her voice edged with urgency and determination.

"I understand the risks, Aoife," I said, my voice quivering with emotion. My eyes glistened with unshed tears, and my hands trembled slightly.

"I wanted to protect you both from this, that's why I didn't tell either of you about it," I said, choking on the words as they left my mouth. The weight of what Aoife had just told me pressed hard against my chest, and I stifled a sob that threatened to break free. My mind reeled with the idea that I might fail not only Son, but Nina too. The unyielding ache of that knowledge made my shoulders tremble as I struggled to hold back the flood of tears. I had never thought it would come to this, that desperation would make working with Aoife the only chance I had left. My breath caught in my throat, and I clung to the fragile hope that I could still make it right. I needed to. Wiping my eyes with the back of my hand, I steeled myself to focus, to take in every detail of Aoife's plan. Surely, we had a chance if we moved quickly enough, or I wouldn't live with the alternative.

"Pay close attention," she whispered, Aoife's voice barely audible over the hum of the bustling city.

"They know you don't have the data on you, and you've concealed it well. Tomorrow, on Friday, precisely at seven o'clock in the evening, make sure to place it in the trash can beneath the old, iron train clock right near Gare de l'Ouest."

"You'll get a call before the drop," Aoife explained, her voice steady and unyielding. "You'll confirm that you have the package in your possession and that nobody's following you. Once you place the package exactly as instructed, you must leave the scene immediately. Any hint of hesitation, interference, or clever manoeuvres, and she will die," Aoife declared, her words as sharp as a blade.

"If they check the file and find it authentic, she'll be set free," Aoife elaborated, her gaze fixed and unwavering. "But if there's a mistake, even the smallest one, she won't be," she added with a chilling finality.

"I need proof that Nina is alive and OK before I do this," I stated.

"Laura, you have no other option." The words hang in the air like a death sentence. Suddenly, my phone vibrates with a piercing urgency. I snatch it up, my heart pounding like a war drum. The screen lights up with a chilling image. Nina was there on the screen, captured in a single, haunting moment. Her wide eyes brimmed with terror, a look that pierced straight into my core. They had her, just as Aoife had warned. Her hands were tightly bound, the cruel constraints biting into her skin. Each rope seemed like an accusation, a reminder that I was powerless to help. The room around her was stark and shadow-filled, the walls cold and indifferent. She sat on the floor, a discarded figure against the darkness, the harsh glare of a single bulb casting deep shadows across her face. A gag was tied over her mouth, silencing her screams, her pleas for help. The image was as brutal as it was clear: Nina was alone, vulnerable, and at their mercy.

"Do you believe me now?" Aoife enquired.

"Yes, I do," I responded.

"What about you, Aoife? Will they—?" My voice cracked under the weight of unspoken fears, each word like a raw wound.

Would I lose her too? Everything felt dangerously out of control. The thought pressed in on me, suffocating. My mind raced, careening through the possibilities, each more terrifying than the last. Losing Aoife, losing Nina. The spectre of it clawed at me, leaving me breathless.

"Just do what they want, and everything will be okay!" she commanded, her voice unwavering, a powerful mix of desperation and authority that pierced my frantic thoughts. The sharpness of her words left no room for doubt, demanding action, demanding compliance. The urgency was palpable, a force that sharpened the air around us. I saw the stakes in the fierce determination of her eyes, and my heart clenched at the realisation of how fragile this hope was—how easily it could all fall apart. My breath came in ragged gasps as I imagined the unthinkable, my mind conjuring images of losing them both, of being left with nothing but guilt and regret.

"I need to leave now; they're watching me as well. It's not just you who's at risk," Aoife said, glancing over her shoulder. Her words were clipped, brimming with urgency, and they came at me like a rush of cold air. I saw the tension in her posture, the way she held her body alert and ready to move. Aoife's eyes scanned the street; their lively curiosity now edged with caution and fear. My heart tightened at the sight of her like this, so unlike her usual vibrant self. It hadn't hit me fully until now just how deeply she was involved, how much danger she faced. Her voice, usually warm and inviting, had taken on a brittle, hurried quality that told me everything I needed to know she was scared, and she might not have much time. The realisation that she could be followed, caught, or worse struck me like a physical blow. I knew she was risking everything to help me, and just like Nina, she might not make it through this alive.

Aoife turned to leave, her slender figure already fading into the flow of people. I felt an overwhelming sense of panic rise in my chest, a fear that this might be the last time I would ever see her. Her blonde hair streamed behind her, catching the light in a way that made her look both fragile and determined. In seconds she was part of the crowd, a moving shadow swallowed by the city. It happened so quickly and so quietly that I was left stunned, reeling from the speed of it all. For a moment, all I could do was stand there, frozen, with the realisation that she was gone. The world seemed to narrow around me, the noise of the bustling street fading into a dull roar. Aoife was gone, and I was completely alone once again. Only this time, the stakes were higher, and the urgency of the situation was more dire than ever before. My fingers fumbled. I wasn't trained for this — I was improvising with every breath.

I had to admit that what I'd feared was true: I had no one else to rely on, no other cards to play. The desperation of my situation was almost suffocating, pressing in on all sides as I watched the place where she disappeared. Indifference seemed to hang in the air, a city alive with everything but concern for my predicament. She was right. I truly had no other option.

Chapter 34

Aoife's warning resonates in my mind. "Nina's in danger." The phrase plays over and over, like a needle stuck on a record, scratching at my thoughts.

I place the phone down and press my palms against my eyes until patterns of colour form behind my eyelids. A metallic taste lingers in my mouth. My shoulders are sore from being tensed for so long.

Feeling isolated and aware of the challenging task awaiting me the next day, I pick up the phone and unlock it.

I type, delete, and type again.

Salut, how are you?

Delete.

I am sorry, I am in danger (déranger), but I need your help (aidez-moi S'il vous plaît).

Is it too dramatic? Too vague? Delete.

My fingers fly over the keyboard before doubt can take hold again.

"C'est Laura. êtes-vous à la maison? Je t'expliquerai quand je te verrai."

II press send before my courage leaves me.

I could only hope they understood the message, despite my clumsy French. Then three dots appear, vanish, then reappear. I felt my chest tighten. I check the phone again.

Nothing.

I imagined them staring at the message, either puzzled or irritated. Perhaps they're busy. Maybe—

Then the phone buzzes in my hand.

Salut, l'adresse est 322 Rue du Noyer, Appt 3B. Je suis à la maison ce soir.

I finally release a breath that I didn't know I was holding. My eyes were burning with relief, but there's no time for tears.

I emerge from the metro station into the cold night air, my breath forming small clouds that dissipate too quickly. Keeping my head down, face half-hidden by my collar, I scan the street without looking like I was scanning. A couple of months ago I wouldn't have known how to do this. Now, I'm learning fast. I boarded Line 1 at Montgomery, the map etched into my memory now from survival rather than sightseeing.

I take the long route, doubling back twice. Changing direction at the last moment before crossing streets. I check reflections in shop windows. My phone stays off—they could track it otherwise. The address sent is memorised, repeating in my mind with each step. Rue de la Loi. 142. Apartment 3B.

A man in a dark coat exits a bar ahead of me. I quickly duck into a doorway, counts to twenty. When I emerge, he's gone. Coincidence or threat? Impossible to know.

Brussels at night feels different now. The city that once dazzled me with its golden architecture now offers too many shadows, too many hidden corners. The waffle shops and chocolate stores where I'd treat myself on weekend afternoons are shuttered and grim behind metal grates. I miss the person I was not long ago. Before the files.

I spot the building across the boulevard—a narrow five-story structure wedged between a bookshop and a closed café. Older than its neighbours, with wrought-iron balconies and tall windows. I studied it from the shelter of a bus stop. No suspicious vehicles parked nearby. No one loitering at the entrance.

Still, I watch and wait, then count to one hundred.

I cross the street, keeping my pace casual. My hair, freed from its usual neat style, hangs limp around my face after hours in the rain. I hadn't changed clothes since fleeing and can't remember the last time I ate.

The building's entrance is recessed from the street, a small alcove with an ornate door and a panel of buzzers. Each labelled with names or numbers. 3B.

I glance over my shoulder. A couple walks arm in arm on the opposite sidewalk, laughing. A delivery cyclist pedals past. No one pays me any attention.

My finger hovers over the buzzer. Once I press it, there's no turning back. I'll have to explain everything. Ask for help. Trust someone I barely know with information that might get them both killed.

I press the button.

The intercom crackles. Silence.

"Hello."

"Bonjour, c'est Laura," I say, my voice sounding strange to my own ears. Hoarse. Thin.

Another beat of silence. Then a buzz—so loud it makes me jump. The lock on the door clicks.

I push through into a small, tiled lobby. A row of mailboxes lines one wall. A potted plant droops in the corner, underwatered. The air smells of old cigarettes and something cooking garlic and tomatoes, warm and inviting against the cold dread that's been my companion all day.

No elevator. A narrow staircase curves upward.

I begin to climb, my footsteps echoing despite my attempt to move quietly. My legs feel heavy, the adrenaline that carried me across the city finally ebbing away, leaving exhaustion in its wake.

First floor: closed doors, the sound of televisions behind them.

Between the first and second floors, a small window looks out onto an interior courtyard, pitch black at this hour.

Second floor: a bicycle chained to the banister, a child's drawings taped to a door.

By the time I reach the landing of the third floor, my breath comes faster. Not from exertion—from fear. What will they say? How much should I reveal?

The hallway is dim, a single bulb casting yellow light over two doors. 3A and 3B.

3B is at the end of the hall. White door, looks recently painted but not in a good way. A small peephole at eye level.

I stand before it, raising my hand to knock, then hesitating. I straighten my jacket, pushing my hair back from my face. Ridiculous to care about appearances now, but some habits persist even in crisis.

From inside, footsteps approach. A shadow passes across the peephole.

I hold my breath.

The door opens, revealing Luca. Seeing him feels like stepping from shadows into dazzling light. He doesn't dominate the space with his size, but with an undeniable presence, standing casually yet attentively. His eyes lock onto mine right away.

He's just as I remember, yet somehow more. His shoulder-length hair is pulled back, a few strands escaping to frame his face. He's barefoot, wearing faded jeans and a simple grey t-shirt that clings just enough to suggest the lean strength beneath.

A dishtowel is slung over his shoulder—he's been cooking, the scent of basil and garlic clinging to him.

"Laura," he says, my name softened by his accent.

That crooked smile appears—left side of his mouth lifting slightly higher than the right, the smile doesn't reach his eyes, though. They remain serious, assessing.

The last time I saw him flashes through my mind. Coffee in the Grand Place, now here I am, on his doorstep, bringing danger to his door.

"I shouldn't have come," I begin to say, but the words die as Luca reaches forward, his hand hovering near my arm without touching.

"You're shaking," he says.

I am? I look down at my hands. They tremble visibly. How long have that been happening?

Luca studies my face, and I wonder what he sees. My hair hangs limp around my shoulders. My eyes feel swollen and raw. There's a coffee stain on my blouse from this morning—a lifetime ago.

He doesn't ask questions. Not yet. Instead, he steps back slightly, making space for me to enter. An invitation without pressure.

The hallway feels suddenly cold compared to the warmth emanating from his apartment. Or maybe that's just him— Luca has always radiated heat, as though his Neapolitan heritage burned just beneath his skin, regardless of how long he's lived in the grey Belgian climate.

I notice his hands—long-fingered, strong, with a fresh burn mark on the right thumb, probably from cooking. Chef's hands.

His eyes never leave me. They're brown, but in this light,

flecks of amber catch the glow from the apartment behind him. There's concern there, curiosity, and something else—a watchfulness that makes me feel both exposed and protected.

The smile shifts, growing even gentler.

"Did you manage to find the place okay?" he asks in his broken English, as if her unexpected appearance at his door in the middle of the night were entirely ordinary. As if they had simply planned to meet for dinner and she had arrived right on time.

"Laura," Luca repeats, this time infusing my name with warmth. He steps forward, puts his hands to rest on my shoulders, both gentle and assured. Then he leans in—the customary European greeting, yet it feels different now. His cheek grazes mine, left side first, the evening stubble lightly scratching my skin.

The aroma of him reaches me: olive oil, basil, a hint of wine, layered with something unmistakably Luca, something I had buried deep in memory. His lips briefly press near my ear before he shifts, repeating the gesture on my right cheek. Although the contact lasts only seconds, it anchors me after hours of fear and fleeing.

Behind him, his apartment glows with warm light. I catch glimpses—bookshelves stuffed with paperbacks, a guitar leaning against the wall, a half-set chess game on a coffee table. The normality of it seems almost obscene against the chaos of my current life.

Steam rises from something cooking on the stove. The mundane domesticity of it nearly breaks me.

When he steps back, his hands remain on my shoulders in a steadying hold. His eyes study my face, moving from my tangled hair to my pale cheeks and finally to the set of my tense jaw. His expression changes, the polite smile giving way to something more serious, more intent.

"You're in trouble," he states flatly, not as a question.

That simple admission shatters something inside me. After a day spent hiding, pretending, and learning that my friends were in peril, my lower lip trembles before I bite it to hold back tears.

"Yes," I manage to reply.

Luca nods once with finality. "Come in," he says, stepping aside. "Have a drink. No matter what it is, something warm in your hands might make things clearer."

He gestures toward the heart of his apartment. As I step past him, the threshold takes on a significance I can hardly explain. The door clicks softly behind me, a subtle barrier between me and the danger pursuing me.

Inside, the apartment unfolds before me, larger than I had anticipated, with lofty ceilings and tall windows overlooking the street. The furnishings form an eclectic mix: a well-worn leather sofa adorned with a vibrant hand-woven blanket, bookshelves assembled from wooden crates, and artwork on the walls that ranges from classic film posters to what appear to be original sketches. Potted plants crowd the windowsills, flourishing despite the meagre Brussels sunlight.

A pot simmers on the stove in the open kitchen to my right. Whatever he's cooking carries the comforting aroma of home, of safety. My stomach clenches, a sharp reminder of just how hungry I was.

"Listen, why don't you take a shower and freshen up before eating?" Luca suggests, opening the bathroom door and handing me a towel along with some of his own clothes to change into.

"Your English has really gotten better," I say with a smile.

"I've been, how do you say, learning," he replied.

Quietly, I took the clothes and bath towel from him and walked into the bathroom, shutting the door behind me with a gentle click. It wasn't long before the steam from the shower began to envelop the room, curling around me like a warm embrace. Stepping into the shower, the hot water cascaded over my face, a soothing torrent that washed away the day's tension. I stood beneath the steady stream, feeling each droplet as it drummed against my skin, savouring the blissful warmth that seeped into my bones. Time seemed to dissolve, and I lingered there, lost in the comforting cocoon of heat and water for what felt like an eternity.

I towelled myself off and dressed in the clothes Luca gave me: an oversized t-shirt and jeans that were too large for me but much too small for him. I wondered if it belonged to a previous female companion.

As I stepped out of the bathroom, the warm, inviting glow of the room drew my eyes to Luca, who was gesturing me over to the table with a welcoming smile. The table was artfully set: two elegantly curved wine glasses stood ready, gleaming in the soft light. Beside them lay a few rustic slices of crusty baguette, their golden edges promising a satisfying crunch. Two large, empty bowls awaited the meal, their pristine surfaces hinting at the feast to come.

I settled into my seat, and Luca began to pour a rich, ruby-red wine into each glass, the liquid swirling and catching the light as it filled the bowls of the glasses. The air was soon infused with its deep, fruity aroma. With a flourish, Luca brought over a large, steaming platter. It was heaped with delicate fettuccine, each strand gleaming with a light sheen of olive oil. Nestled among the pasta were vibrant baby tomatoes, their skins glossy and taut, and fragrant basil leaves scattered generously, their bright green hue adding a fresh, aromatic touch to the dish.

"Mange, s'il te plait," he requested.

"Merci, Luca." I lifted my glass to clink it with his. For the first time in ages, I felt like I could finally breathe, even if just for a moment. My fingers fumbled.

"I wasn't expecting to see you again," he commented, reclining in his chair while sipping his drink, anticipating my response.

"I'm sorry," I began. "Let's just say things with my host family have been difficult."

I gazed over his apartment again, taking in details I missed at first. A small table in the corner had papers spread across it, handwritten pages, a laptop, books. A photograph on the wall shows Luca with an older couple, perhaps his parents? All standing before a blue ocean. Naples, maybe.

I know so little about him, really. Yet I'm here, trusting him with everything.

"Ce n'est pas important, you're here now," he says. His eyes catch the lamplight, warm and steady. "Whatever it is."

"I think someone wants to kill me," I say.

Chapter 35

"They are not coming here," Luca says, his voice steady. "Brussels is large. Nobody will find you here."

I look up towards his eyes. "You don't know who 'they' are."

"No." He takes a sip of wine. "But I know fear when I see it. And I know sometimes, the right question is not who, but why."

My appetite dims. I place my fork down carefully. The pasta congeals. "I worked as an au pair for a typical French family. I knew it was going to be an adventure, but not this," I say finally. The words feel dangerous in my mouth.

Luca doesn't push, just nods. Waits.

"I found something," I said quietly. "Files I was never meant to see and now they are after me."

"And they know you saw?" he asked.

"Yes." My hand trembles as I reach for more wine.

Luca's hand slides across the table, stopping just short of mine. An offering, not a demand. "You are safe here."

The phrase sounds hollow, a promise too big for anyone to keep —but his eyes hold steady, and I find myself wanting to believe him and I lift my hand to his.

"Eat," he encourages. "Food first, fear second."

A small laugh escapes me, surprising us both. "Is that another one of your Nonna's sayings?"

"No, that one is pure Luca." He grins, breaking the tension. "My Nonna would say something more like 'a full stomach makes the devil sleep'."

We eat in a comfortable silence. I manage another half plate before the knot in my stomach tightens again. Luca clears the dishes without comment, returns with a small plate of store-bought tiramisu and two forks.

"Not homemade," he apologises. "But acceptable."

The dessert is rich, coffee-soaked ladyfingers and mascarpone melting on my tongue. I watch Luca's hands—strong, capable, a small burn scar on his left thumb. He catches me looking and flexes his fingers playfully.

"Chef hands," he explains. "Many battles with hot oil."

"How long have you been in Brussels?" I ask, steering toward safer shores.

"Five years. After Naples, then Rome for a while. Brussels was not planned, but..." He shrugs. "Life happens where you are standing."

"And the café?"

"Ah, Café Milano," he said, a hint of fondness in his voice. "Funny thing—the owner's actually from Sicily, not Milan at all. But a good man. Gave me a job as head chef when things were... well, complicated." He gave a small, wavering motion with his hand, as if the word didn't quite cover it.

I nod, understanding the unspoken. "And now?"

"Now, all is correct. I am also the manager when Giuseppe is away. I have a home." He gestures around the apartment. "Small, but mine."

"It's nice," I say, meaning it. "Feels lived in."

"This is good, yes? A place that feels like someone lives there, not just exists."

Something about his phrasing strikes me. How long have I merely existed in my parents' Dublin home? Going to work, coming home, watching the same shows, reading the same types of books. Safety in routine. Back then, danger was something that happened to other people.

Fat lot of good it did me.

"What will you do?" Luca asks, his voice gentle but direct.

I push the dessert plate away. "I don't know. The company has government contracts. Deep pockets."

"And long arms."

"Yes."

Luca leans back in his chair, studying me. "You could disappear. New name, new place."

"They have my friend; I can't let them get away with it." The force in my voice surprises me.

A smile spreads across his face, not amusement, but something like admiration.

"This is the real Laura, I think. Not the frightened one who came to my door a couple of hours ago."

Heat crawls up my neck. "Both are real. I'm terrified. But I'm also... angry."

"Anger is fuel," he says. "Fear is the brake. You need both to drive safely."

The metaphor is unexpectedly perfect. I feel something shifting inside of me, something beyond the immediate attraction to this kind, perceptive man, far different to the Italian that I met not so long ago.

He reaches across the table again, and this time, I meet him halfway. Our fingers intertwine. His palm is warm against mine. "But not tonight. Tonight, you rest."

The touch grounds me in the present moment. His thumb traces small circles on my skin.

"I've put you in danger," I whisper. "Just by being here."

"I choose this danger." His eyes don't waver. "Some things are worth the risk."

The air between us changes, charges with something beyond words. I become acutely aware of my breathing, the slight parting of my lips, the way Luca's gaze drops to notice.

He stands, still holding my hand, gently pulling me to her feet. We face each other in the soft lamplight, close enough that I can smell the wine on his breath, the faint citrus of his cologne.

"Laura," he says, my name transformed by his accent into something musical. "Whatever comes, you are not alone now."

The weight of those words settles around my shoulders like a blanket. How long have I been alone? Not just these terrifying days on the run, but before—in my ordered, empty life.

I don't consciously decide to step closer. My body makes the choice for me. His arms open, enfolding me in warmth that feels both foreign and familiar. I tuck my head against his chest; ear pressed to his heartbeat. Steady. Certain.

His hand strokes my hair, tentative at first, then with more assurance when I don't pull away. We stand like this, swaying slightly, as if to music only we can hear. The danger waiting outside these walls recedes, not gone but momentarily held at bay by this fragile connection.

When I tilt my face up to him, the question in my eyes is answered before it's asked. Luca's lips find mine with gentle precision. The kiss is brief, a question of its own, giving me space to decide. I answer by rising onto my tiptoes, hands sliding up to frame his face, pulling him back to me with newfound certainty.

The second kiss deepens, crosses a boundary from comfort into desire. His hands span my waist, fingers pressing just enough to indicate hunger held in careful check. I can taste coffee and wine, feel the slight scrape of evening stubble against my chin. The sensation is electric, awakening nerve endings dulled by days of fear.

When we separate, both breathing harder, Luca rests his forehead against mine. "Stay," he murmurs. Not a command but an invitation.

I know he means more than just tonight, more than just his bed. He's offering a foothold in my free-fall, the threat still looming— none of it has changed. But something fundamental has shifted in how I can face it.

"Yes," I whisper against his lips. "I'll stay."

His smile is an overwhelming force, a tidal wave of warmth that crashes between us as he kisses me again, this time with a fierce urgency that demands attention. His hands move down my back with a grip that's both commanding and gentle, as he lifts me effortlessly against his solid frame, revealing a strength that takes me by surprise. I wrap my legs around his waist, feeling the powerful rhythm of his determined strides as he carries me down the narrow, dimly lit hallway toward the bedroom, the air charged and pulsing with anticipation with each step.

The bedroom is enveloped in a cloak of shadows, a haven of tranquility disturbed only by the rhythmic symphony of our mingled breaths. The air is thick with anticipation as our lips collide in a fervent embrace, and our hands move with an urgency akin to a storm, deftly removing the layers of clothing that separate us. Luca pauses momentarily, his eyes locking onto mine with a piercing intensity that sends a thrilling current through my veins, making my heart pound like a distant drum. He trails fervent kisses over my eyelids, cheeks, and neck, each touch a gentle yet insistent caress that sends shivers down my spine, pulling me irresistibly closer to him. In an almost dreamlike trance, the world around us fades away, and we find ourselves stripped bare, our bodies seamlessly interwoven in a heated, intimate dance that blurs the lines between reality and fantasy.

Every breath, every touch feels magnified in the quiet room, like time has slowed just for us. Luca's hands move over me with purpose—slow at first, exploring, learning. His fingers trail lightly along my collarbone, then down my side, leaving a warm path in their wake. When he cups my waist, his grip is firm but careful, as if he's afraid I might disappear.

He smooths his hands across my back, his thumbs drawing small, steady circles against my skin. They drift lower, tracing the curve of my hips, and I feel my breath catch. There's a quiet intensity in the way he holds me—not demanding, but certain. His touch says everything he isn't putting into words.

I hold onto him, my own hands searching, anchoring. He presses a kiss to my neck, murmurs my name, and I shiver. The air around us is warm and heavy, but it's his touch that keeps my heart pounding.

As we move together, his hands never leave me—sliding, holding, steadying—making me feel like I'm exactly where I'm meant to be.

Tomorrow will bring new dangers, difficult decisions. But tonight, in this small Brussels apartment with its mismatched furniture and perfect pasta, I find something I thought lost forever. Hope. Connection. And the surprising discovery is that when running for your life, sometimes you run directly into exactly what you need.

Chapter 36

His eyes open. No gradual awakening—just sleep, then consciousness, dark eyes fixing on mine immediately.

"Buongiorno, Bella." His voice carries the roughness of sleep, but his smile forms instantly, as if he's been practising it in his dreams.

"Morning." My voice catches, still surprised by the intimacy of waking beside him after just one night together.

Luca stretches, the sheet sliding down to reveal the constellation of freckles across his shoulders. "What time is it?"

I glanced at the ancient clock radio on his bedside table. "Ten."

"Merde." He sits up, hair falling loose around his shoulders. "Paolo will have my head. I told him I'd open up by twelve for the lunch service."

I prop myself on one elbow, watching as he swings his legs over the side of the bed. The muscles in his back shift as he reaches for the hair tie on the nightstand. I feel a momentary urge to reach out, to trace the line of his spine with my fingertips but I don't.

"The café will survive without you for another hour." I say, trying to keep my tone light

Luca glances over his shoulder as he ties his hair back in one swift, practiced motion. "Maybe so," he says, a faint smile tugging at his lips. "But the lunch rush won't take care of itself." He pauses, eyes meeting mine. "Truth is, I'd love nothing more than to spend the whole day in bed with you, Laura."

The comment lands like a pebble in still water, small but creating ripples. I shift, pulling the sheet higher.

"I have—" I started, but he cut me off.

"—Things to do. Yes, I remember," he said, already walking over to the dresser. "Very important things that make you glance over your shoulder every five minutes."

The apartment feels smaller suddenly. It's not large to begin with—a one-bedroom above a spice shop in the Matonge district, filled with mismatched furniture and the lingering scents of Luca's experiments with Belgian-Italian fusion cooking. But it's safe. Safer than I've been in a while.

"I'm careful, not paranoid." The lie tastes stale.

Luca pulls a fresh shirt from a drawer. "There's a difference?" His tone remains playful, but his eyes sharpen. "Stay here today. I'll bring back something special from the café."

I didn't answer. His hand finds mine, warm and solid. A cook's hands, nicked with small scars from knives and burns, but gentle. I feel momentarily anchored.

He studies my face, reading something in my expression that makes his smile fade. "These people you're running from—"

"I never said I was running."

"You didn't have to." He squeezes my hand.

Heat rises in my cheeks. I thought I was being so subtle.

"My apartment isn't much, but it's secure. Stay here. Rest." He tucks a strand of hair behind my ear, the gesture casual but his eyes intent. "Just today. Please."

The temptation pulls at me like gravity. Sleep without nightmares. A day without looking over my shoulder. But the weight of the flash drive, hidden in the lining of my jacket hanging by the door, seems to grow heavier with each second.

"I need to go out for a couple of hours, but I could come back.

After."

Luca's expression shifts—relief mixing with concern. "I'll be done at eight. We could have dinner here or meet me at the restaurant and I'll make something especially for you."

"I'd like that." This, at least, is not a lie.

He leans forward, pressing his lips to my forehead. "Be careful out there, Bella. Brussels isn't always kind to beautiful mysteries."

I feel a tightness in my chest, an uncomfortable heat that I recognise as guilt. Guilt because I'm dragging him into my chaos. Guilt because I'm already planning the quickest route to the pedestrian bridge. Guilt because after the drop, I might not come back at all.

Luca pulls away, finishing the buttons on his shirt. "There's coffee in the kitchen. And bread from yesterday—still good with some of that jam Paolo's mother sent."

"Thank you." For the coffee. For not pressing further. For creating this bubble of normalcy that I can pretend to inhabit.

He disappears into the bathroom. Water runs. A razor taps against the sink. I sit motionless in the bed, calculating times, distances, and contingencies. The drop at the bridge needs to happen at exactly seven o'clock. Which means smiling goodbye to Luca and promising to return, knowing that promise might dissolve like sugar in rain.

When he emerges, hair now neatly tied back and face freshly shaved, I'm already dressed and pouring coffee into the chipped mug he left on the counter for me —the one with a faded map of Naples on its side.

"So efficient," he teases, but his eyes track my movements with new awareness.

I hand him his keys, our fingers brush, and I feels a spark—static from the dry air, but it jolts me nonetheless. Luca closed the apartment door with a soft, decisive click that echoed gently in the quiet hallway.

Alone in the apartment, I inhale deeply to collect my swirling thoughts, savouring the cool morning air that gently caresses my skin through the open window. The crisp freshness mingles with the rich, comforting aroma of my steaming cup of coffee, creating a serene moment of clarity and reflection. Resisting the urge to linger in the comforting warmth of the apartment, I quickly dress, the fabric of my clothes feeling familiar and grounding. Soon after, I slip out, leaving behind the stillness and stepping into the bustling world beyond.

The stairwell smells of cardamom and cloves from the spice shop below, familiar after just after a night of sanctuary. I descend quickly, trying to ensure my footsteps are light on the worn steps. The flash drive presses against my hip from its hiding place in my jacket lining, small but significant, like a pebble in a shoe that might start an avalanche.

Outside, Brussels greets me with thin sunlight and the distant rumble of trams. I pulled a knit cap low over my ears, more for anonymity than warmth. I take the long route to the bridge, doubling back twice. I stop at a corner store to buy nothing, just to check the reflection in the security mirror. No one follows. Or no one I can spot.

The pedestrian bridge spans the canal, connecting the trendy boutiques of Saint-Géry with the grittier immigrant neighbourhoods beyond. Neutral ground. My contact had been chosen well.

The drop point: a rusted public trash bin at the midpoint of the bridge, third slat from the bottom where the metal has warped to create a small hiding space. Simple. Anonymous. Fifteen seconds to complete if uninterrupted.

My phone begins to vibrate. A message from an unknown number:

"Confirmation still expected at scheduled time."

I don't reply. Not breaking stride, the bridge stretches before me, thankfully empty save for a cyclist disappearing at the far end. Perfect. I'll be there in forty seconds. Thirty-nine. Thirty-eight.

Then I hear them.

Laughter explodes onto the bridge from the western entrance , a crash of voices and stumbling feet. Six, maybe seven young people spill onto the walkway, arms linked, voices raised in fractured songs. The group staggers forward in a loose cluster. A tall woman wearing a plastic tiara tipped at a precarious angle gesture wildly, nearly taking out a shorter companion's eye. "It's my hen night, bitches! I want to go to all the bars in Brussels!"

They're blocking the centre of the bridge. Right where I need to be.

The bride-to-be plants herself directly beside the trash bin, leaning against the railing. "This spot is perfect! Everyone get in!"

There is a collective shuffling as phones emerge, screens lighting faces from below. The girl with the tiara arranges them, directing like a film auteur. "Michelle, you're too tall; crouch down a bit. Emma, on the other side. No, the other side!"

I stopped fifteen feet away, trapped in the open. Too close to turn back without drawing attention. Too far to complete the drop. I begin to look at my phone, pretending to check messages, hyper-aware of the seconds ticking by.

The girl in the tiara leans dangerously far over the railing, posing with the canal as backdrop. Her friends lean with her, a row of bodies exactly where I need access.

"Come on, Siri, take the damn photo already!" someone calls.

"It's on timer! Ten seconds!"

I glanced at my phone again, it was 6:57. Three minutes until drop time. I could force my way through, but that would be memorable.

Standing out is the last thing I want right now. They snap their photos and will begin to head to their next destination, I suppose.

I couldn't believe it, here's my chance. I managed to quietly dispose of the data in the trash, ensuring that no one noticed. But then I felt the weight of observation prickling across my skin. My steps don't falter, but my awareness sharpens, focusing outward like a camera lens adjusting. That's when I spot him. Standing at the far end of the bridge, a man in a charcoal coat watches me. Not the casual glance of a passerby, but the fixed attention of purpose. His stillness amid the flow of pedestrians marks him as clearly as if he wore a sign. He's waiting for someone. He's waiting for me.

He was of trim build. Close-cropped hair. Unremarkable features that slide from memory even as I observe them. His hands remain in his coat pockets, holding something? A generic black scarf circles his neck. Everything about him is designed to blend, to be forgotten by witnesses. Everything except his stillness and his focus.

He's a professional. Someone's cleaner, perhaps. Someone sent me to retrieve what I'm planting, or was he there to retrieve me?

The man shifts his weight slightly, angling toward my path. He hasn't approached yet, which means he's either waiting for confirmation or backup. Neither option gives me much time.

Twenty feet separate us now. His gaze hasn't wavered. My fingers curled around my phone, ready to dial the emergency number, not that police would arrive in time to help.

Fifteen feet.

Ten.

Then, from behind me, an explosion of laughter and stumbling footsteps—the hen party group, having abandoned the canal-side drama, now spills toward the western exit of the bridge. The same exit the man in the charcoal coat blocks.

"Next venue!" the tiara-wearing bride to be girl announces, voice carrying across the space between them.

The man's focus breaks, his gaze flicking toward the approaching noise with professional assessment. His shoulders tense slightly, he wasn't expecting this disruption to a clean retrieval.

The hen party group surges forward, a wave of celebratory chaos washing toward the man. The bride-to-be, with the infallible social radar of the inebriated, zeroes in on him immediately.

"Hey! Serious man! You look like you need a hug!"

I begin to watch the scene unfold. The man takes half a step back, hands emerging from his pockets, trying to create distance.

"No thank you," he says, voice neutral but firm.

The girl is undeterred. "Come on! One photo with the bride-to-be! For luck!"

Her friends circle around him, not threatening but overwhelming in their enthusiasm. The man's training is evident in his response—no sudden movements, no escalation, just measured discomfort as he tries to extricate himself without creating a scene.

"I'm waiting for someone," he says.

She faces me while standing in the centre of the bridge and

responds, "We'll be quick!"

One of the girls is already positioning herself next to him, phone ready. "Just one selfie and we'll let you go back to being mysterious and handsome."

The man's eyes dart past the group, he sees me still standing at a distance. Our gazes lock for three precise seconds. Message received: he knows me, and I've seen him before too. This interruption changes nothing.

The bride-to-be grabs his arm. "Phone ready! Everyone say 'Brussels!"

The man allows a tight smile, professional enough to know that resistance creates memorable scenes. I quickly use his momentary distraction to retreat into a café doorway at the end of the bridge. Through the window, I watch the group of girls surround him completely, phones raised, tiara glinting in the sun.

I slip inside, moving quickly through the tables to the back hallway where a restroom sign points the way. Three minutes later, I emerge from the service entrance into an alley that runs parallel to the main street.

I turn left at the next corner, then right, establishing a pattern before breaking it. Surely the man in the charcoal coat will have extracted himself from the group of revellers by now, I thought.

Chapter 37

A few hours earlier, laughter erupts from a group of women clustered around a high table; their faces flushed with alcohol and celebration. The bride isn't hard to spot, her plastic tiara catches the dim light, throwing tiny reflections against the wall like nervous stars.

Time is of the essence; I order a gin and tonic that I have no plan to drink and wait. Twenty minutes later, the bride excuses herself from her friends and heads to the bathroom. I follow her, and we meet at the sink while she's adjusting her outfit.

"Are you enjoying your hen night?" I enquire as the bride's eyes meet mine in the mirror, mascara slightly smudged at the corners, creating shadows that make her look both vulnerable and dangerous.

"We sure are," she responded cheerfully.

"Would you like to earn a quick five hundred euros for ten minutes' work?" I ask.

"What, are you serious?" she says as she turns to look directly at me.

"It would be a great story to tell people about your hen night, wouldn't it?" The bride nods with enthusiasm, then returns to her lipstick application as if nothing happened. Up close, she's younger than I expected. Maybe twenty-five, twenty-six.

"You're paying me to spy on someone," she says.

"No, I'm paying you to help me put something in his pocket without him noticing it," I correct her.

The bride-to-be laugh is sharp enough to cut glass.

The celebration tiara is tucked into carefully styled hair.

Designer dress that probably cost a month's rent. Engagement ring that costs considerably more. But there's something in her expression that doesn't match the occasion.

I reach into my pocket and place a small device on the bathroom table between us. It's no larger than a coat button, black and inconspicuous. The bride stares at it.

"And here is five hundred euros," I say, sliding a sealed envelope across the bathroom sink. "You slip this into his pocket when I give you the nod. That's all you need to do."

The bride's fingers hover over the envelope for a second before taking it. She doesn't open it, just tucks it into her purse with practised discretion.

"You're the only one who needs to get close enough to him," I say, leaning forward slightly. "You're the bride-to-be."

She picks up the tracking device with manicured fingers, examining it. "Where does this need to go?"

"Inside pocket. Left side if possible."

"And after I plant it?"

"Nothing. Go back to your celebration. Enjoy your night." I keep my voice steady. "I'll take care of the rest."

She tucks the device into her purse, next to the envelope. "I don't need to know." The bride stands, smoothing down her dress. She adjusts her tiara with a practised gesture and smiles at herself in the mirror.

For a moment, the bride looks like she might say something else. Then the bathroom door bangs open, and a giggling bridesmaid calls out.

"Amelie! We're doing shots! Where are you hiding?"

Amelie transforms instantly. Her shoulders relax, her mouth

curves into a practised smile, her eyes light up with manufactured excitement.

"Yes, and after that we're off to another bar," she explained.

And just like that, it's done. I watch her go, the small tracker now in Amelie's possession, the deal sealed with five hundred euros and no questions asked. The unspoken truth hangs between us.

I leave my untouched drink and exit through the back door. The night air is cool against my face, carrying the smell of rain and city grime. Later that evening, the tracker will activate and I'll finally have a direct line to Pierre and Nina. I just have to survive until then.

The signal pings just after it's planted, sharp and insistent on the phone screen. I sit up straight on the hard bench, eyes narrowing at the small red dot now moving steadily across the digital map of Brussels. The tracker is working. My breath fogs in the cooling air as I watch the dot crawl north through the city grid.

The tracker, now embedded deep in the stranger's coat pocket, shows a slow but steady movement north through the city. He hasn't noticed. Either that, or he doesn't care.

I sit on a bench at Botanique station, pretending to flick through social media on my phone while the dot inches toward Rogier. No one notices me. I've perfected the art of blending in, of becoming just another face in Brussels in recent times.

He's on foot—or more likely, using the metro. The dot's smooth, steady progress suggests public transportation. I descend the stairs into the station. The familiar smell hits me: damp concrete, electricity, perfume, bodies. The underground pulse of the city. I boarded Line 1 at Montgomery, the map etched into my memory now from survival rather than sightseeing.

I board the next train, line two, slipping into the back corner where I can keep an eye on both the exits and the map. The carriage isn't crowded, just enough passengers to provide cover without obstructing my view. An elderly woman clutches a shopping bag to her chest. Two businessmen stand near the door speaking rapid French about quarterly reports. A teenager with headphones stares blankly at the floor.

The fluorescent lights flicker, casting strange shadows on blank faces. Brussels moves around me in fragments, blurry faces, murmured French and Flemish, the stale smell of damp wool and city grime. The train rattles north, stopping at Rogier where half the carriage empties and refills with new bodies, new smells, new concerns. The doors slide shut. I checked my phone again, the dot is ahead of me now, moving toward Yser.

I lean back against the hard plastic seat, trying to look bored, disinterested. Inside, my heart pounds against my ribs like something trying to escape. This is the closest I've been to Pierre and his associates since seeing him outside the house in Ixelles.

The train slows again. Yser station. The doors open with a pneumatic hiss.

That's when I see him.

Grey coat. Broad shoulders. Even from behind, his stance carries authority—controlled, alert. He steps onto the platform with quiet precision, moving like someone who knows what it means to be followed. Then he turns, just slightly, pretending to study the station map. That's when I know. The scar over his left eyebrow. The same hard line to his jaw. It's him. The man I saw speaking to Pierre that night—when I came back early from my day trip and caught them outside the front door.

I wait until he's halfway up the stairs before following, always keeping two people between us, a man in a business suit, then a group of tourists. Distance is crucial. If he notices me now, everything is lost.

He exits the station and heads toward the canal district, abandoned warehouses, quiet alleys, and rows of squat brick buildings forgotten by city planners. I follow at a distance, hood up, hands in my pockets. The evening is getting colder, darker. Streetlights cast pools of sickly yellow on wet pavement. Few people walk here after business hours.

They pass a row of closed shops, dark windows shuttered. A homeless man huddles in a doorway, wrapped in layers of grimy blankets. A cat darts across our path, disappearing into an alley. The canal appears ahead—black water reflecting fractured light from the buildings on the opposite bank.

He pauses at a corner, lighting a cigarette. The flame briefly illuminates his face, sharp features, cold eyes, the scar a pale line above his left eyebrow. I duck into a doorway, heart hammering. He hasn't seen me, I'm sure of it. But something about his pause feels deliberate, as if he's sensing the night air for pursuit.

After a long moment, he continues, turning onto a narrow street that runs parallel to the canal. The buildings here are older, industrial, with fewer windows and more shadows. Perfect for meetings that need to stay hidden. Perfect for exchanges that can't bear witness.

I follow him, keeping my footsteps light, but the gap between us stretches as he increases his pace. I let him gain distance, better to lose sight temporarily than risk detection. The red dot on my phone guides me. He's moving faster now, with purpose.

When I turn the corner, he's gone.

I instantly freeze, pressing myself against the brick wall of the nearest building. My eyes scan the empty street, loading docks, metal doors, abandoned delivery entrances. No sign of him but the tracker shows he's close, very close. I move forward cautiously, one step at a time, alert to every sound.

There—a metal door, slightly ajar, spilling a thin line of light onto the wet pavement. The tracker points directly to it.

I approached the door slowly, keeping to the shadows. No cameras visible, but that means nothing. Places like this, hidden places where men like him conduct business—they have other security measures. I then stop several metres away, weighing up my options. Following him inside would be foolish, possibly fatal. But waiting out here exposes me to other dangers.

So, I chose a compromise, finding a recessed doorway across the street with a clear view of the metal door. From here, hopefully I can watch without being seen. I slid down against the cold concrete, positioning myself in the deepest shadows, and focus on the thin line of light across the street.

Every few minutes, I check the tracker. The dot hasn't moved. He's definitely inside, conducting whatever business brought him to this forgotten corner of Brussels. I pull my jacket tighter around me. The night air carries the smell of the canal—damp stone, algae, diesel. All I have to do now is wait.

The tracker hasn't moved. Whatever happens there, it's taking time. Brussels begins to sleep around me, or at least this forgotten corner of it does. No cars pass. No pedestrians wander by. Just the occasional distant siren and the gentle lap of canal water against stone walls.

A text vibrates my phone. Aoife.

"You OK? I'm worried about you!"

I silence the phone without responding. Aoife means well, but explaining my current situation isn't possible. How do I tell my friend that I'm crouched in a doorway, stalking a man whose associates have already killed someone?

The metal door suddenly swings open. Light spills onto the wet pavement in a bright rectangle. I press deeper into my shadowed alcove, barely breathing.

Pierre emerges first, his collar turned up against the cold. Behind him, the man at the drop-off. They speak briefly, voices too low to catch. The man passes something to Pierre—a small package, perhaps a thumb drive. Then they part, the stranger retreating inside, the metal door closing with a dull clang.

Pierre pockets the item and walks briskly back toward the main road. Should I follow him? I'm torn, but I have to find Nina; Pierre will have to wait.

My phone vibrates. Not a text this time. An alert.

The tracker is moving again. The red dot on my screen descends through the building. I sprint to the corner of the building, positioning myself where I can see both the front entrance and part of the street. I wait, my breath held, my muscles tense.

A flicker of movement. The side door creaks open. He steps out, dragging something behind him. A tarp. My stomach is clenched. He pauses, scanning the shadows. I shrink into the crumbling brick, the chill seeping through my clothes.

The interior is worse than I expected—dark, damp, and choked with silence. I pull out my phone. The tracker blinks steadily: she's close. Basement level.

I spotted a stairwell across the room, mostly collapsed but passable. I descend slowly, avoiding the centre of each step, creak less there. Below, the air is different, colder, thicker, almost metallic.

I reach a corridor of storage rooms, doors ajar or broken off entirely. I move past rows of rusting filing cabinets and cracked cement pillars. Then I saw her.

Nina is in a chair, duct tape at her wrists, blood dried at her temple. She's dazed, but alive. Her eyes lock on mine—widening in shock, then fear. She mouths a word: behind.

Too late.

Footsteps. Fast. Close. A shadow slices across the far wall.

I dive behind a stack of crates just as the man enters, flashlight scanning. He steps into the room, raised gun, muttering curses.

"I know you're in here."

My hand grips the pocketknife in my jacket. My heart pounds so loud it could give me away.

A phone vibrates in his pocket, catching his attention. He picks it up, a bit preoccupied.

"Hello? Yeah, I'm aware she's left; she's been trailing me?"

As he briefly turns away, I make my move.

Two strides, low and fast. I drive my shoulder into his back, sending him crashing into the wall. His flashlight clatters to the floor, spinning wildly. Shadows leap like phantoms. The gun—where is it?

He spins, grabs my jacket, and we go down hard. My head snaps back against concrete; stars bloom in my vision. He's on top of me, snarling, breath sour with sweat and something metallic.

"Wrong night to play hero," he growls, reaching for something behind his back—a knife, maybe.

My fingers find my own. I jab upward blindly, catching flesh. He roars and rolls off me, clutching his side.

I scramble to Nina. The tape tears away with a sound like ripping flesh. She winces but tries to help me, pulling at her own bonds once her hands are free.

"We have to go—now."

But the sound of footsteps echoes again. Not just one set. Two. Maybe more. Reinforcements.

"No time for the stairs," I cry.

There, a broken grate, leading into a crawlspace, maybe maintenance tunnels. I pry it open, heart hammering.

She hesitates, looking back. "What if they follow?"

"They will," I say, shoving her gently inside. "So, we make sure they follow me."

I toss her my phone. "Go. Follow the tunnel. Signal if you reach the street."

She disappears into the dark without another word. I jam the grate halfway closed behind her.

Footsteps now just down the hall.

I grab the flashlight from the ground and throw it hard down the opposite corridor—it bounces, crashes, draws attention.

Then we run.

Heavy boots thunder after me. Shouts now. One voice was angry. One calm, too calm. The man I stabbed is still moving, I can hear the wet drag of his injury as he yells, "She's not alone!"

I hit the stairwell two at a time, back to ground level. I don't know the building—I don't need to. I just need to keep them away from her. Long enough.

I burst through a rusted door into the loading dock. Empty space. No cover. I sprint.

Nina's right behind me, limping but moving fast. I grab her hand, and we sprint into the open, boots slapping against wet concrete. The air is heavy with rain coming, sky bruised purple and black above.

Behind us, the door crashes open again.

"GO!" I shout.

We veer around a pile of scrap pallets, ducking low. Bullets snap past us—too close. One punches through a metal drum inches from my head. We don't stop.

The chain-link fence at the edge of the lot comes into view— tall, but climbable. I boost Nina up, hands slick with blood and sweat. She scrambles over, drops to the other side with a grunt. I follow, my boots scraping, ribs aching.

I hit the ground hard on the other side of the fence, the impact jarring up through my knees. Nina's already moving, limping but determined. I grab her hand again and we sprint down a narrow alley choked with garbage and broken glass, lungs burning.

Behind us, the screech of sneakers on wet pavement. Shouts.

They're still coming.

"Left!" I pull Nina down a side street, nearly slipping on the slick cobblestones. The city looms ahead like a mirage, streetlights, noise, life. If we can just make it another block.

We break out onto a busier avenue, traffic, people, headlights. For one perfect moment, we're invisible. Just two soaked figures among a dozen others hurrying through the rain.

Then, Nina stumbles.

I catch her before she hits the ground. "Come on," I breathe. "Stay with me." My fingers fumbled.

I dash into the street, waving both arms. The driver honks and nearly swerves around us—but stops. I yank the back door open and shove Nina inside.

The driver blinks at us. "You bleeding?"

"I'll tip big," I say. "Just drive."

"Where to?"

I rattle off an address—somewhere safe. For now.

As the cab pulls away, I glance out the rear window.

A figure stands at the edge of the alley, watching. He doesn't run. He doesn't shout. He just stares.

Then he raises a hand—not to wave, but to point. Right at me.

I sink into the seat, heart still hammering.

Nina leans on my shoulder, whispering, "Is it over?"

I don't answer.

Because I know it's not.

Chapter 38

The cab lets us out a couple of blocks away, near a dim row of terraced houses. I assist Nina as she exits, shielding her from the brunt of the wind. The rain is easing, but everything is thoroughly drenched. Her boots squish with each step she takes.

We slip through a side gate into the garden of number 41, then head to the back, where a narrow laneway leads us to a separate entrance, small and discreet. It's an annex with its own kitchenette and bathroom. This is where Aoife resides.

Before we can knock, Aoife opens the door. She must have been peeking through the blinds. She immediately embraces Nina, pulling her into the warmth inside.

"You're soaked to the bone," she says, pulling us both indoors.

The space is a tight one bedroom, a futon, and a counter cluttered with mugs and open notebooks. Laundry hangs on a radiator, and a half-eaten apple sits on the table. The air smells of instant coffee and rain.

"My host family is in Lyon for a wedding," Aoife says, handing us towels. "They won't be back until Monday. You're safe here."

Nina settles onto the futon, shivering but alert. Her face appears pale under the yellow light, her eyes shadowed. I sit beside her, still feeling tense.

That's when I hear the subtle creak of a floorboard behind me.

I whip around swiftly.

Joseph emerges from the dimly lit bedroom, holding a steaming mug of tea that sends wisps of aromatic vapour curling into the air.

"You look like you've been through the mill, are you both OK?" he remarks with a half-smile that doesn't quite reach his eyes.

I freeze in place, my heart pounding.

Aoife darts her gaze between us, her expression a mix of relief and apprehension. "I called him. I figured you'd need help," she explains, her voice soft yet reassuring.

I nod slowly, my eyes fixed on Joseph, who stands there with a composed demeanour, as if our presence is no surprise to him. He doesn't ask what happened, doesn't express any shock or concern, just stands there as though he's been waiting for this moment.

"You shouldn't be involved in this," I declared, my voice laced with a blend of concern and suspicion. The gravity of the situation weighed heavily on my words as I thought about the many people who had already been placed in harm's way. My eyes narrowed slightly, reflecting the unease that had settled in my chest, while the tension in the air seemed to thicken with each passing moment.

I scrutinise him with piercing intensity, my gaze dissecting every subtle inconsistency like a scalpel. There's something disturbingly off about his forced nonchalance, a brittle facade that seems ready to shatter. The way he conspicuously avoids any enquiry into Nina's or my wellbeing is like a glaring spotlight on his disinterest. His eyes flicker incessantly toward the door, a nervous tic that betrays a crack in his supposed calm, as if he's expecting an unwelcome visitor at any moment. Meanwhile, his phone sits on the table beside him, its screen lighting up repeatedly like an incessant alarm, casting a pale glow that dances across his face. Yet, despite the persistent illumination, he doesn't even spare it a glance, as if ignoring a fire alarm in a burning building.

"We barely made it," I say, my voice a low, controlled tremor. "They were moving her. Almost as if they knew I was coming."

A suffocating silence hangs in the air like a storm cloud about to break.

Then Joseph responds, curt and dismissive. "Lucky break."

Nina, lying on the futon with exhaustion etched into her features, lifts her head, her voice a raspy whisper growing stronger. "One of them said a name. Pierre."

Aoife stiffens, her gaze piercing me like a dagger as she tries to tend to Niina's injuries. "Pierre? Your employer Pierre?"

"That's the one," I reply with grim certainty.

"Is he somehow involved in all of this?'" Aoife asks.

"Yes, he is. Listen, guys, I need some fresh air. I'm just going to step outside for a moment to clear my head," I explained, feeling the room's walls closing in around me.

"I'll join you," Joseph says as we step through the main entrance, the soft click echoing in the dimly lit hallway behind us.

That's when I notice it, a barely visible flinch, like a shadow passing over his features, but unmistakably there. Now he's avoiding eye contact, his fingers twitching like restless spiders near the phone, betraying the turmoil beneath his calm exterior.

I step forward, feeling the air grow thick with tension, a heavy cloak draping over us. "How long have you been working with him?" I ask, my voice is steady but edged with suspicion.

Joseph exhales, the sound weary and filled with unspoken burden. His demeanour is heavy with resignation, as if the weight of his secrets is pressing down on him. "You have no idea what you're involved in," he replies, his voice barely above a whisper.

I nod, a single, deliberate gesture that cuts through the charged air. "Then tell me," I urge, my curiosity mingling with a growing sense of dread.

Joseph remains silent, the unspoken truths suspended between us like a fragile web.

Suddenly, he moves with startling speed, his actions fluid and without hesitation. One arm snakes around my throat, the cold steel of a knife pressing against my skin, while the other twists my arm behind my back, immobilising me.

"Don't resist," he murmurs in my ear, his voice low and filled with urgency. "It'll only make things worse."

With a swift and decisive motion, Joseph yanks open the back door of a sleek, black car that has mysteriously appeared in front of the house—I could swear it wasn't there when we first arrived —and promptly pushed me inside. The leather seats are cool against my skin as he settles in beside me, pulling the door shut with a firm and final click. Instantly, we're cocooned in the car's interior, as the outside world blurs into an indistinct tapestry of shapes and colours. The door slams shut behind us, enveloping us in a deep, shadowy darkness that feels both isolating and secure.

No headlights cut through the darkness, and the windows are blacked out, making the vehicle an ominous silhouette. Just waiting.

Pierre is inside, sitting regally in the centre as if he owns the place. His black coat is impeccably tailored, the fabric catching the dim light, while his gloved hands exude an air of authority. Each strand of his hair is meticulously in place, a testament to his composed demeanour.

"Bonsoir," he greets me with a smooth, almost familiar tone, as if we're old friends meeting for a casual drink.

Pierre's eyes scrutinise me for a brief moment, a glint of amusement in their depths. "You're persistent, I'll give you that," he remarks with a hint of admiration threading through his voice. "I respect that. But persistence comes with a cost."

I fix him with a fierce glare. "You won't get away with this."

"Oh, I already have," he replies, his voice smooth and assured. "But you? You have a choice to make."

Chapter 39

Joseph crouched low, his movements swift and precise, like a man long accustomed to working in silence. His fingers closed around the zipper of a weather-beaten duffel bag resting between his feet. The faint rasp of the zip echoed in the dim interior of the SUV, a small sound that somehow rang with enormous consequences. The bag's opening yawned, revealing its secrets: a sleek black laptop with smudged fingerprints across the lid, a thick manila envelope bulging with documents, and a matte-black flash drive no larger than a piece of gum.

Each item was unassuming. Ordinary, even. But they radiated tension—like live wires humming beneath the surface, each one capable of detonating lives with a single click.

Outside, the SUV drifted through the unseen veins of the city, those narrow arteries most citizens never noticed. It wove through shadow-choked underpasses, skirting the edges of abandoned railyards and forgotten industrial parks where graffiti sprawled like warnings and rust painted every surface. Derelict warehouses with shattered windows watched from the shadows, silent sentinels to clandestine meetings and deals made in darkness. This was a part of the city that had learned to keep its mouth shut.

Pierre sat still in the backseat; one leg elegantly crossed over the other. He looked out the tinted window with an air of amusement, then turned toward me, his mouth curling into a cold, deliberate smile, the kind that never touched the eyes. His smile was polished, but it didn't reach his eyes. 'You ask a lot of questions, Laura,' he said. 'Curiosity can be dangerous.'

"An unrelenting investigator," he began, his voice smooth as silk stretched over broken glass, "decided to poke around in places he shouldn't. My wife, ever trusting, was approached. They tried to use her. Turn her into a mole."

I tensed up, unsure where this was going, but Pierre's gaze never wavered.

"She ran. Took the children. Paris." His lips thinned. "And just when I thought the damage was done, I learned the most exquisite twist of all, she was having an affair with him." He smiled faintly, not with sorrow, but relish. "Irony's an exquisite poison."

He leaned forward slightly, as if sharing a toast. "But that chapter's closed. Let's talk about you."

Joseph powered up the laptop. The hum of the machine filled the vehicle. A cold, artificial light flared across his face, casting shadows that made him look like a ghost in a digital graveyard.

"Cyberterrorist. Government informant. Industrial saboteur," Pierre said slowly, savouring each label like a fine wine. "You're a masterpiece of corruption. And by dawn, you'll be a global villain."

The screen displayed an image—me. Mid-step. Blurry but unmistakable. A freeze-frame from surveillance footage: the night Son was killed, in a cheap motel lobby, my face partially turned, expression unreadable.

Splayed across the screen in bold red:

SUSPECT IDENTIFIED IN GLOBAL CYBER ATTACK
LAURA FARRELL LINKED TO MASSIVE DATA LEAK
GOVERNMENT SYSTEMS COMPROMISED — HOMICIDE POSSIBLE

Below it, screenshots of doctored emails, digital blueprints of the breach, and crypto transaction logs cleverly tying my name to offshore wallets. The level of forgery was astonishing— terrifyingly thorough.

I swallowed hard, my pulse hammering in my throat. "I didn't —"

Pierre waved a hand, cutting me off. "Of course you didn't. I did. But when this bomb explodes, guess who'll be holding the shrapnel?"

His grin widened. "The NSA. Interpol. Even Beijing—they're all eager to meet you. You'll be hunted across continents."

Joseph chuckled. A low, scratchy sound that made my stomach lurch. He was enjoying this. All of it.

Pierre's voice dropped to a whisper. "We plant the drive, leak the evidence, and the media takes care of the rest. Your face will be on every screen by morning."

But what Pierre didn't know—what neither of them realised— was that I had seen this trap forming long before tonight. Beside the seat cushion, my wrist pressed against my watch band. A faint click. Barely audible. But enough.

The signal was sent.

A dormant drone, parked two blocks away in a nondescript delivery van, stirred to life. Its rotors whispered into the night as it rose silently, carrying a payload of encrypted logs, timestamps, footage, and exact coordinates—broadcast-ready and targeted to trusted journalists, watchdog organisations, and cybersecurity units across three continents.

The transmitter on my wrist had already done its job, sending a silent pulse into the air like a digital flare. The drone was enroute, loaded with everything: footage, logs, the breadcrumb trail I'd setup while pretending to stumble blindly through Pierre's elaborate trap. I only needed to stall.

So I played along.

"Do you really think this plan will work?" I asked, voice

deliberately flat, careful not to give away the firestorm building behind my ribs.

Pierre tilted his head, studying me with that unnervingly calm expression of his—like a man admiring his reflection in a dark mirror. His fingers moved lightly over the keyboard again, tapping commands with the assured ease of someone who believed in the infallibility of his own design.

He smiled faintly. "It's not a plan anymore, Laura. It's reality. A carefully crafted one, with you cast in the starring role." His eyes gleamed. "This isn't a theory being tested. It's a verdict already delivered."

My heart pounded in my chest, steady but loud. I could hear it in my ears, feel it in my fingertips. I forced my jaw to stay loose, my breathing even. No clenched fists. No darting glances. Not yet.

Pierre leaned forward slightly, as if sharing a secret. "What you're experiencing now—that sense of helplessness? It's what most people feel too late. After their name is already ruined. After they've disappeared into the system."

His words were smooth, clinical, and almost rehearsed. He wanted me to feel small, boxed in, defeated.

But I wasn't defeated.

I was counting.

Ten seconds passed. The drone would be clearing the rooftops by now, guided by GPS, silent and fast. I pictured its sleek, black, almost insect-like, wings slicing through the dusk, invisible to the naked eye.

Twenty seconds.

Pierre's voice had turned indulgent. He was basking in his monologue, explaining how he'd rewritten reality with code and precision and lies. He thought I was paralysed by fear.

I wasn't.

Thirty-five seconds.

I nodded slowly, feigning reluctant understanding. "And after they arrest me—what then? What's the endgame for you?"

He grinned, pleased I was finally asking the "right" questions.

"Simple. You're erased, and I walk away clean. The scandal consumes you, not me. I'm a victim. A man whose system was exploited by a reckless saboteur."

Fifty seconds.

The glow from the laptop screen flickered over his face like firelight—casting shadows that made him look almost demonic. Joseph hadn't moved, still catching his breath, oblivious to the countdown underway right under his nose.

I smiled then. Just slightly. Enough for Pierre to notice. His smile was polished, but it didn't reach his eyes. 'You ask a lot of questions, Laura,' he said. 'Curiosity can be dangerous.'

"Something funny?" he asked, narrowing his eyes.

I looked up, calm now.

"Just that you think I ever stopped playing."

Sixty seconds.

The sky above us buzzed—soft at first, then louder. Pierre blinked, confused, turning toward the sound. Through the window, the blinking red eye of the drone came into view, hovering just beyond the glass.

And in that moment, his expression cracked.

I moved. Fast.

Pierre's brows lifted in smug amusement. "It's already working."

That's when I struck him. I spun, my elbow driving hard into Joseph's throat. He wheezed, clutching his neck. I didn't wait, I grabbed the laptop and slammed it against the dashboard. Sparks shot from the shattered screen as shards of plastic and wire sprayed across the car's interior.

Pierre lunged. Too slow.

I kicked at the SUV door. Locked.

Above us, the drone buzzed into view, its red status light blinking. It hovered; camera locked onto the vehicle. Pierre froze. His face was drained of colour.

Broadcast: LIVE.

The truth—the real truth—was already uploading.

I looked at Pierre, breathing hard. "You always believed you were the smartest in the room," I said.

He stared, speechless.

"But you never paid attention to the walls."

Chapter 40

That's when the car slammed into us from the side with a ferocious, bone-crushing impact that reverberated through every inch of my body. The sound of steel crunched with an ear-splitting roar, reminiscent of thunder cracking open the sky, while shards of glass erupted into the air like deadly shrapnel, glinting in the harsh sunlight. The world twisted violently, a nauseating blur of colours and shapes, transforming into a kaleidoscope of destruction that seemed to spin endlessly. Metal shrieked in agony, a high-pitched wail, as it tore into the rear quarter of our car, its claws of chaos forcing the driver—a hulking brute with more muscle than skill—into a desperate, erratic veer. The vehicle fishtailed wildly, tires screaming like tormented souls being dragged to the abyss, until we collided with a line of trash bins, coming to a bone-shattering, teeth-rattling stop that reverberated in my bones. My head snapped forward with brutal force, smashing against the window, sending a dazzling cascade of stars exploding across my vision, each one a testament to the violence of the impact.

Then I heard it—doors bursting open with a metallic clang. Boots thundered on the asphalt with a frantic urgency, a relentless drumming that sent my heart into a frenzy.

"Hands where I can see them!"

The commands cut through the chaos, sharp and clear as a bell. The driver, his instincts dulled by desperation, reached for something under his jacket, a fatal mistake. A loud crack split the air like a whip, echoing ominously. He slumped forward, lifeless and still.

The passenger door was yanked open with a forceful tug, and a gloved hand reached in, firm and unyielding. "We've got you," the officer barked, his voice steady and reassuring as he pulled me out. "You're safe. You're safe."

High above us, a drone hovered in the pale afternoon sky like a mechanical sentinel, its tiny rotors slicing through the air with an ominous hum. The sleek, unblinking eye of its camera remained locked on every movement, capturing the chaos below with cold precision. This wasn't just surveillance, it was a live broadcast, feeding real-time footage to screens around the globe. Somewhere, in homes, offices, and control rooms, strangers watched our desperate flight unfold—eyes glued to the drama, hearts racing not because they were in danger, but because we were.

I staggered to my feet, my legs trembling and unsteady like a newborn colt finding its balance, as another officer took hold of my arm with a steady, reassuring grip, guiding me to the curb. The once unmarked van now stood in stark clarity, its true identity unveiled by the bold insignia emblazoned across its side, the letters of Interpol gleaming with authority in the early morning light.

The tactical unit had arrived, a synchronised force moving with precision and purpose. They had come through, just in the nick of time, their presence, a shield against chaos.

And Pierre? He was pinned against a cold, unyielding wall across the street, his wrists encircled by the unforgiving bite of handcuffs. His voice, filled with futile anger, echoed into the void, words lost to the wind, ignored by all who had more pressing matters to attend to.

Justice didn't always come with a trial. Sometimes, it arrived with flashing lights, authoritative voices, and a global feed that broadcast the truth for all to see.

"Laura, are you OK?" a voice called out.

It was unmistakably Alex standing in front of me. For a moment, everything around us—the sound of the city, the tension in my chest, even the flicker of panic—seemed to pause. My fingers fumbled. I wasn't trained for this — I was improvising with every breath.

Earlier that day, I had taken a risk. I didn't know how else to reach him safely, so I sent a short, coded message: a time, a location, and a simple request. If you get this, track me. Watch. Listen. No complicated instructions. Just a plea he would understand if he still trusted me.

I had no way of knowing if it had worked. No reply. No confirmation. And in the time since, I'd prepared myself for the worst—being on my own, being hunted, and possibly disappearing without anyone ever knowing the truth. But now, here he was.

And more than that, above us, hovering just beyond the rooftops, was a drone. Small, dark, barely noticeable to anyone who wasn't looking for it. But I saw it immediately. That was the sign. Our sign.

He'd understood. He'd come.

A rush of relief swept over me, so strong I nearly staggered. He had gotten the message, read between the lines, and acted. Quietly. Carefully. The way I knew he would if he still believed in me. My eyes met him. I didn't need to say anything—not yet. Everything I couldn't say aloud was already written in the tension of my shoulders, the dirt on my clothes, the fear I was trying to keep buried.

And his face—calm, steady, alert—told me I wasn't alone anymore.

He hadn't just shown up. He had planned. Prepared. He was already in motion.

"Finally, you made it," I remarked, striving to keep my voice steady and composed despite the adrenaline coursing through my veins.

"You're welcome," Alex responded with a smirk. "Just like we planned. You owe me a bottle of something very expensive."

"You still had the file?" I asked, a hint of relief seeping into my voice.

"Of course," he replied confidently. "I knew you'd manage to get yourself into a bind. I was already tuned in before the car door even closed."

My mind went back to Aoife and Nina.

"Are Aoife and Nina alright?" I enquired; my voice strained with concern as tears started to fall down my face.

"They're just over there," Alex indicated, as he stepped to the side pointing at the police car they had just exited.

Chapter 41

The story broke across Belgian news outlets late that afternoon: Marceau Duval, CEO of Cipherion Global, had been formally charged in connection with the death of Canadian au pair Erin Blake, whose remains were discovered buried in a walled garden at his private estate in Uccle. For weeks, speculation had surrounded her disappearance, but the grim confirmation sent shockwaves through Brussels' political and tech elite. Duval, long considered untouchable within the city's upper echelons was taken into custody under heavy security. Authorities declined to comment on how long Erin's body had been hidden or what had led them to the property, but sources close to the investigation hinted at digital evidence and a possible whistleblower from within Cipherion's inner circle. One file stood out: 'CleanupProtocol_04.'.

The police station monitors flickered with a breaking news banner:

"Marceau Duval, CEO of Cipherion Global, apprehended at his Uccle residence in connection with the concealment of a body and a multi-million-euro breach of classified government systems."

Footage played on loop—Duval's grand, detached house surrounded by armed officers and forensic teams, their presence a clear indication of the gravity of what had been uncovered.

I remained still within the stark, institutional confines of the police station, where every noise carried an authoritative echo. My attention shifted to the interview room as I heard the handle turn, and the door opened with a soft creak. Instead of the detective, Camille emerged into the dimly lit hallway. Our eyes met immediately, her expression a blend of relief and resolve. The fluorescent lights gently illuminated her features, accentuating the slight tension in her shoulders as she stepped through the doorway. The air between us felt charged, heavy with unspoken words and unanswered questions.

Camille looks composed, her coat draped neatly over her arm, her hair pinned back without a strand out of place. I, by contrast, feel cracked open, my breath shallow, my body taut with waiting.

Neither of us speaks at first.

Then Camille crosses the space between and sits, not too close. In her hand is a sealed envelope, thick and slightly bent at the corners. She sets it down between us on the bench like a loaded weapon.

"I thought you might like this," Camille says quietly.

I ignored the envelope and focused on her instead, noting the calmness in her voice and the heavy weight she bears with such grace that it's almost imperceptible.

"Why did you leave me in Brussels all alone?" I asked, my voice straining under the weight of hours spent in turmoil. Part of me wanted to understand, clinging to the hope of a reasonable explanation, while another part simmered with resentment, unable to shake off the sense of abandonment.

Camille's eyes flicker, but her face remains unreadable.

"My children mean the world to me, and I would do anything to protect them, you have to understand that." she stated.

I gaze down at the envelope, my fingers hesitating before I finally tear it open. Inside, a Polaroid peeks out, capturing a fleeting, joyful moment frozen in time. The photograph shows a sunlit Montmartre balcony, where Max's grin stretches from ear to ear, full of warmth and mischief. Beside him, Chloe's cheeks are flushed with a rosy hue, her eyes sparkling with laughter and the vibrancy of the moment. The backdrop of the city adds a touch of romantic nostalgia, as if the scene itself is whispering tales of carefree days and cherished memories.

"I took Max and Chloe to Paris for their safety," Camille insists, leaning in, her whisper almost lost in the busy police station. "I've been feeding evidence to the authorities ever since."

My hand closes tightly around the photo's edges, grip tightening. Camille meets my gaze, an uncharacteristic vulnerability flickering beneath her polished surface.

"I was terrified," she confesses, her voice trembling slightly, each word meticulously chosen as if she were balancing on a razor's edge. "I couldn't let Pierre discover I was aiding you. The danger was too great, and it was safer for him to believe you had nothing to do with it at all."

My hand touches the Polaroid again, her thumb brushing over Chloe's tiny, reaching hand. Everything feels so fragile, like it might shatter if she breathes too hard. My fingers fumbled.

"You were aware of the risk I faced," I accuse, my voice just above a whisper.

We both remained silent for a while, the quiet between us dense —not with anger, but with unsaid words.

"I have to leave," she murmured.

"I know," I replied.

She stepped closer and gently placed a hand on my shoulder, her touch light and cool, almost hesitant. A tired, fleeting smile passed through her lips, more sadness than comfort.

She turned toward the front door, then paused and glanced back.

"I wish things had turned out differently," she said quietly.

"So do I," I said.

And that was the end.

No embraces, no dramatic farewells. Just the quiet departure of two people who had experienced too much, trusted too little, and now had to go their separate ways.

As she descended the front steps to the street, she didn't glance back.

****

The kitchen buzzed with a subtle intensity, knives clinking, pans crackling, and the soft exchange of orders being given and acknowledged. Luca was stationed at the pass, his sleeves rolled up and apron marked with stains, a towel draped over his shoulder. He moved with precise concentration, carefully plating a sea bass with citrus beurre blanc, verifying the garnishes, and sending it out with a nod.

"Luca, il y a quelqu'un pour toi," one of the waiters explained.

It was right in the midst of the dinner service, a bustling scene with clattering dishes and the mingling aroma of roasted meats and freshly baked bread filling the room. He was engulfed in the flurry of activity, surrounded by waitstaff weaving gracefully between tables and guests engaged in lively chatter. Time for pleasantries was a luxury he couldn't afford at that moment; another customer was wanting to either compliment or complain about the food, he could never tell which it was going to be. But curiosity got the better of him and he looked up.

Through the open line, just beyond the heat lamps and swinging doors, he looked at me.

I stood by the host stand, my clothes quietly dripping from the rain, surveying the room with uncertainty about whether I fit in. My coat remained buttoned, and my eyes bore the unmistakable weariness of someone who feels pursued. Yet, here I was.

Luca froze for just a breath—then turned to his sous-chef.

"Take the pass."

He wiped his hands, pushed through the swinging door, but stopped just short of the dining room, staying within the shadows near the kitchen.

As I caught sight of him, my heart quickened, and I moved closer, watching his every step as I approached him.

He pointed to the closest vacant table, stepped out from the kitchen door, walked onto the floor, and presented me with an empty table.

"I figured you weren't just being polite when you said you owed me dinner," I said, voice low, teasing—but brittle at the edges.

"I wasn't," he said. "You hungry?"

I nodded. "Starving. For something real."

"I'll send something out. No menu. You'll eat what I make."

My eyes met his gaze, and for the first time in weeks, my shoulders eased just slightly.

"That's exactly what I was hoping you'd say."

Luca turned back into the kitchen, the doors swinging shut behind him. One of the waitresses poured me a glass of white wine as he instructed her to do so. Not long after, the first dish landed at my table, a plate that said more than words ever could.

The aroma hit me first: bright, citrusy, and tinged with the subtle scent of the sea. Resting on a warm plate was a delicate fillet of branzino al limone, its skin crisped to a golden finish, the flesh tender and glistening beneath. A drizzle of lemon-infused olive oil pooled around the edges, mingling with slivers of garlic and a handful of capers. Steam rose gently, carrying whispers of fresh parsley and cracked black pepper, light, elegant, and bursting with coastal simplicity. A wedge of lemon waited on the side, like a final touch of sun. It was the kind of dish that made you feel looked after. As if someone had thought about every detail—not just to feed you, but to reach you.

And as the rain tapped softly on the windows outside, I took my first bite.

Warm. Real. Safe.

For the first time in a long time, I wasn't looking over my shoulder.

Printed in Dunstable, United Kingdom